Russell  *ed*
the line of *ft*
off.

"Did you ...ow a single extortionist, burglar, arsonist, vandal, bank robber or graffiti artist before you married Todd Howard?" Esther asked.

"Of course not," Laura said.

"How about white collar crime? Did you ever date someone who was into fraud? Identity theft? Forgery? Cybercrime?" Esther asked.

"You left out counterfeiting," Russ said.

"My mistake."

"I'm not sharing my dating history with you two," Laura told them. "You two make it sound like I recruit criminals as a hobby. It's not that bad."

"It's that bad," Russ said quietly.

"Except for the little trouble we had at the Street of Dreams . . ."

"Three murders and a kidnapping?" Russ asked, verifying Laura's definition of "a little trouble."

". . .my life has actually been relatively calm," she continued.

"Relatively?" Russ repeated. "You took down a bank robber!"

"That was the other guy's idea."

"There's no need to be modest. You knocked him out cold."

Studs, Tools
&
Fools

Kathleen Hering

Published November 2015
By Kathleen Hering
Albany, Oregon

.

ISBN-13: 978-1515222651
ISBN-10: 1515222659-

for

Kitty

1

The paunchy security guard at the bank was six months away from retirement. He was completing his thirty-seventh year on the job and he couldn't recall a day when he hadn't enjoyed his work. It was a peach of a job.

He worked at one of the few banks in the country that still had armed guards posted, and, he suspected, even the customers realized the weapons were mostly for show. He hoped he'd get through this last stretch of his career without having to fire the damn thing. He had never been sure he could shoot someone if the occasion arose. He'd worried about this since his first day of employment here, but the perks that came with the job made it worth the risk.

Security Guard Frank Thomas liked to look at women. It was as simple as that. He spent every hour of his work day watching young women employees and bank patrons come in and out. And, he got paid for it.

He thought Portland, Oregon, had a greater degree of sophistication than the rest of the state. Local news agencies labeled the city "trendy," while some residents relished in calling it "weird."

It struck Frank Thomas as odd that no citizens had demanded that the bank guards stash their employer-issued guns in the back of the bank vault. It was just a matter of time.

Downtown Portland was populated by what Frank and his contemporaries called "career women." Toward the end of each month the number of these stylishly-attired women visiting the local bank increased. Frank suspected some of them were there to transfer funds to cover what they'd overspent on their designer clothing purchases.

He was paid to watch everyone entering the bank, but it was these women who drew Frank Thomas' attention. Their wardrobes, their confident strides, and their assured smiles. . . And, each of them smiled at him and thanked him for holding the door open.

This wasn't the first time Frank noticed the pretty, auburn-haired woman who approached the door. Oh, to be twenty years younger, he thought. He did a quick calculation and yearned to be thirty years younger.

Laura Howard stopped by the bank twice a month. And she never failed to smile at him. He predicted any day now that some young Portland businessman or attorney (there seemed to be an adequate supply of the latter) would sweep her off her feet and Frank would see their wedding photo in *The Oregonian*.

She was tall and thin and had an air of spunkiness about her, he thought. It was in her stride. It was in the way her hair swept across her forehead and behind one ear. He estimated that she was about 5' 7", but her calm, confident manner (and a pair of killer high-heeled shoes) made her seem much taller. He'd put her age between twenty-eight and thirty two.

She's friendly, but in control, Frank thought. *She'd* probably have the courage to shoot the damn gun.

LAURA HOWARD was waiting in line in front of the bank teller at the third "customer service station" along the ebony counter. She hated, abhorred, detested, and loathed standing in lines. Today her aversion to waiting was more intense than usual.

Standing in line for her turn on the monkey bars in kindergarten had been tolerable. Filing through the high school graduation line twelve years later had at least been symbolic of an accomplishment. As an adult, Laura recognized that most lines were caused by incompetence at the front of the queue. She particularly hated lines at the bank because she had to pretend she wasn't listening to other customers' business. From two feet away.

Laura wondered if there was a support group for others who shared her dislike for marching in place. Impatience Anonymous? Shufflers Without Partners? She'd probably have to stand in line to register for the group.

She heard a scuffle behind her, and a loud noise echoed through the bank.

Was that a shot? she wondered.

"Everyone down on the ground!" a man yelled.

"In a white suit?" Laura protested.

"What'd you say?"

"Don't shoot. I said 'don't shoot,'" she told the man coming toward her with a gun in his hand.

A little dirt was probably better than a bullet hole and blood stain on the lapel of her new waist-length jacket. She got down on the tile floor with the other customers and the security guard who had been knocked to the floor.

4

"On the ground!" the voice demanded again. The man grabbed the elderly lady who had been in front of Laura in line and threw her to the floor. The woman's cane rattled as it hit the tiles and slid onto the carpeted area beyond her reach.

"Hey!" Laura yelled before she could stop herself.

The man glared at her. "You say something?"

"Stay!" she yelled, pointing at the elderly woman who was now down and crying quietly.

Laura could have driven to the bank any time during the week, she thought. But she chose today. Big mistake.

The teller was slowly filling the brown paper bag the robber had thrust at her. How long did it take to stuff bills in a bag? If you weren't crying and your hands weren't shaking, Laura thought. She'd give the teller a break. As long as the bank robber had the gun in the bank employee's face, he couldn't shoot the rest of them. True. It wasn't one of Laura's more charitable thoughts, but she was in survival mode. In a new suit. On the floor.

The bank lobby floor was cold and hard. As an interior decorator, Laura would have chosen something more attractive than charcoal grey floor tiles. Maybe a warm beige travertine, she thought.

Her mind had done this before in emergency situations. Wild thoughts ping-ponged about in her head in an effort to distract her and keep her calm in the face of danger.

She strained to look to her right without noticeably moving her head. Her eyes met the fierce dark brown eyes of a middle-aged workman who sat on the floor about three feet from her. Laura thought he was scared shit-less. Or mad as hell. He was almost as frightening to her as the armed man at the teller's station. She wondered absently why he wasn't wearing a warm jacket on this cold Portland morning.

The workman was slowly inching his burly, tattooed arm toward Laura. When his arm was extended all the way, he started rolling his eyes and slightly moving his head. He was trying to tell her something, but she didn't understand the message.

Was he an idiot? If he moved again, he could get them both shot.

He continued with the weird eye movements. He'd glance at her arm (anyway, she hoped it was her arm and not her chest) and then start again with the furtive gestures.

Then, she got it! She edged her arm closer to his until he could almost reach her hand. He inched his arm sideways and grasped her hand. The guy had a grip of steel.

He was one of three customers Laura had noticed in the bank before they'd all followed the orders to get down on the floor. There was her new guy friend squeezing her hand, the old lady, and a thirty-something man in a red blazer. A Realtor? Part of a quartet?

"Thank you for choosing the downtown branch," the teller chirped automatically.

The armed man chuckled and backed away from the teller's window toward where Laura and her strong new BFF were frozen in place. If the robber wasn't careful, he'd trip over them, she thought.

Then, she truly got it.

The robber juggled the gun to his other hand and looked down into the bag full of bills as he took two more steps backwards. In one swift motion, Mr. Workman jerked their joined arms up, creating a human "clothes line." It was swift and efficient. And, maybe deadly. The back of the robber's head hit the hard tile floor with a loud "thunk" and he lay still. Laura couldn't tell if he was breathing.

She watched with horror as blood soaked through the hood of the bank robber's sweatshirt. Her stomach churned. She took a deep breath, rose slowly, and raced for the public restroom so she wouldn't throw up on top of the customers still sprawled across the floor.

SHE COULDN'T return to the lobby wearing dirt from the floor and remnants of her partially digested breakfast. She surveyed the suit. The jacket was a total loss. She slipped out of it, turned the inside lining to the outside, and folded it carefully.

The outside of the jacket had been splattered with bodily fluids, as the ever-cautious Centers for Disease Control would label the half-digested bacon, egg, and beans breakfast burrito. She silently questioned her request for "extra red sauce" at the Taco Bell drive up window earlier this morning.

She left the restroom and glanced toward the customer service area where she saw the bank robber was still on the floor, now being restrained by two male customers.

Laura slipped out the side exit door. She crossed the sidewalk, stepped off the curb, and then jumped back. A small black car roared past her and zig-zagged, back and forth, cutting in and out between the cars in the lane closest to her.

Laura looked both ways twice, as she had been taught in kindergarten.

Her dark blue Toyota Tacoma was parked along the curb in a 15-minute metered space a half block from the bank. She unlocked the truck and slipped in the driver's door. She placed the soiled coat on the black rubber floor mat on the passenger side.

She suspected all three tellers had hit their silent alarm buttons in harmony as soon as they saw the robber go down. She heard sirens growing louder as police cruisers approached the bank. The cops were either responding to the bank, she thought, or trying to catch up with Crazy Guy in the small black car.

Her truck cab flooded with reflected red and blue flashing lights from atop the cop cars that now blocked all the entrance doors to the bank branch. Apprehending a bank robber apparently trumped ticketing a dangerous driver.

Laura re-locked the truck, fed the parking meter a quarter, and moved back up the block. More police had arrived and cordoned off traffic lanes going in all directions around the bank.

She motioned to the nearest cop, indicating that she needed to enter the bank.

"Not today you don't," the officer said. "Can't you see we've got a serious situation here?"

"That's why I've got to get in there," she said.

"Bank's closed, lady."

"But. . ."

"What part of 'clear the area!' don't you get?" he asked. He stood with his right hand on the gun in the holster at his hip.

She opened her mouth to explain and the officer took a step forward.

"Now!" he yelled.

"There's no reason to be rude," Laura told him.

She turned and walked back up the block, again crossing the street to where the truck was parked beyond the area now marked off with yellow and black crime tape. She got in, turned the key, and edged the vehicle away from the curb.

DETECTIVE CHRIS PFEIFER looked up from the notes he was reviewing to see Leonard Roberts walking toward him. Lord help them both if the guy was bringing him another case, Pfeifer thought.

"A downtown bank branch was hit this morning," Detective Roberts said.

"I heard."

"Have you seen the video the guys in Robbery are circulating?"

"I thought they had a suspect," Pfeifer said.

"It was a couple of bank customers who nailed the suspect. Man and a woman knocked him out cold. The problem is," he said, "the woman left the bank before our guys could interview her."

"And?" Pfeifer asked.

"I think you should look at that tape. I'll bet you a buck you can identify the woman."

Pfeifer eased his lanky frame out of the desk chair and walked across the room to where Roberts' computer was set up. Roberts pulled up the video clip and he and Pfeifer bent toward the screen to look at the images.

"Why am I not surprised?" Pfeifer asked.

"She's pretty distinctive, isn't she?"

"If that's not Laura Howard, she has a double in town."

Detective Roberts shook his head from side to side while he watched the video from the bank security camera again. "Why would she do that?" he asked.

"*My* dollar says she's taking this all in stride," Pfeifer said.

"No bet. The odds are too far in your favor on that one."

It would have been a safe bet, Pfeifer thought. He'd interviewed Laura Howard at the time of her husband's death and again during an investigation at the Street of Dreams last year. The woman could be caught in an avalanche, he thought, and she'd get up, brush herself

11

off, and keep going. Anyway, that's what she did the time the cement truck hit her, he recalled.

Pfeifer walked back to the laptop computer on his own desk to pull up the list of addresses and phone numbers he kept of past victims, witnesses and narcs. The Howard woman was listed there twice—and once more at home in his little black book.

"She's probably home. Let's go for a ride," he called across the office to Roberts. They both knew their over-worked colleagues investigating the bank robbery wouldn't mind a little assistance.

Neither man wanted to alert Laura Howard with a phone call before their visit.

"Tile floors are the same 'temp' year round. Cold." — Laura Howard, Interior Decorator

2

The rainy months of January and February were down time for the three who ran Graham Construction. The company was owned by the team of building contractor Russell Graham, his aunt and bookkeeper Esther Graham, and interior decorator Laura Howard. Russ' large dog, Hammer, was in charge of security.

The once struggling business was doing well enough now that the two-month slow-down came as a welcome breather for the three owners.

The construction company operated out of the downstairs rooms of Russell Graham's home in Portland. His Aunt Esther had a small cottage-style apartment above the workshop at the back of the property. The workshop and the main house were separated by a small patch of lawn and a wider, paved parking area.

Laura Howard lived across the street and four houses up. She had been remodeling and redecorating her house for several years, but not making rapid progress. She had to intersperse her own home design projects with the decorating jobs that paid her bills.

LAURA PLANNED to sit by the fireplace with Louise for the remainder of the day and thumb through decorating magazines that had collected during the busy summer and fall months. She was still shaken after her experience at the bank this morning. She knew Louise wouldn't demand conversation. Laura had christened her house "The Harrington" after she found a similar house and floor plan printed in a replica Sears Catalog from the early 1900s.

Louise was an over-sized *male* cat, named after a feisty girl from Laura's elementary school days. He was the first to hear someone step onto the covered porch at The Harrington this afternoon. The orange cat tensed, launched from Laura's lap, and scooted undercover behind the couch. Laura heard the rap on the door ten seconds later.

"Coward," she said to the cat.

Laura wasn't any more eager to entertain guests than the cat was. When she'd returned from the bank earlier, she'd showered and slipped into clean-but-tattered and paint-stained coveralls with a mauve long-sleeved top. She smelled better, but the new look was far from a fashion statement.

She peeked out the front window and was pleased to see Esther Graham standing on the porch. The two women often shared a mid-day cup of tea on these furlough days. Laura glanced out the window a second time to make sure no one else had arrived. Esther stood alone now, tapping her foot impatiently.

Louise was the only one Laura had told about the bank robbery. She was shaken when she returned home and knew she needed to calm down enough to form complete sentences before she talked with Esther and Russ. She remembered now that she also needed to contact the police to report that she had witnessed a crime.

"Screening your guests now?" Esther asked as she walked inside.

Laura ignored the comment and moved to the kitchen to pour an additional cup of vanilla tea. Esther opened her mouth to speak, but Laura interrupted.

"Me first," she said. "Essie, you won't believe what happened at the bank. . ."

Louise yowled to announce the sound of more footsteps on the porch. Laura moved to the living room and stood on tiptoes to put her eye against the peephole in the door. She recognized the two police detectives standing on the porch and knew she was too late to make that call to the Portland Police Bureau.

She led Detectives Pfeifer and Roberts through the living room and back to the kitchen table where Esther was sitting. The two women had last seen the detectives a year ago when Graham Construction rehabbed an Italianate house for the Portland Street of Dreams. Laura didn't want to reminisce about that or exchange small talk today. She hoped the detectives would get straight to the point.

"What's up?" she asked.

"We understand you were in on a bank robbery this morning," Roberts said gruffly.

"How much did she take?" Esther asked.

Detective Roberts cleared his throat and leaned forward. "This is an important police matter," he said. "Ms. Howard, were you or were you not in line at a downtown bank just after 10 a.m. today?"

"She were," Esther answered.

"I were," Laura said. "I mean, I *was*," she corrected. "Is that why you're here?"

"Unless you know another reason we should make an official call on you," he said. He let the silence in the room grow for a few extra seconds, wondering what he might hear if he refrained from prompting the witness.

Pfeifer broke the tension. "Did you leave the bank before the officers on scene could interview you?"

"I left before they arrived," Laura said. "And, when I came back, the cops wouldn't let me inside."

"Not possible," Roberts said.

"Let her talk," Pfeifer said. "What exactly happened, Laura?"

"Can I start with after the robber's skull hit the floor and I knew I was going to throw up?"

"Go ahead. We can fill in the other details later."

"There's not a lot to tell. The whole thing made me sick to my stomach. Especially the blood puddle on the floor," she said. "It was obvious the robber wasn't going anywhere soon." She shuttered at the memory. "I got up from the floor and ran to the restroom, but I wasn't fast enough. I wound up with vomit on the sleeve and front of my suit jacket."

"Would that be a white suit?" Roberts asked.

"It's actually a nice buttery cream light wool number, but I called it white when I talked to the robber."

Roberts sighed and Pfeifer stepped in with the next question.

"So, after you up-chucked on your cream suit in the ladies' room, what did you do?"

"I took the smelly jacket out to my truck and went back to the bank, but a cop at the door wouldn't let me back inside."

"And?" Roberts asked.

"I drove home," she said.

"Did you tell the officer you had witnessed a crime?"

"He wouldn't let me tell him anything."

Roberts looked irritated.

Laura was about to tell him that she had planned to call the Police Bureau as soon as she had calmed down at home, but Detective Pfeifer spoke first.

"Let's move on," he said.

"OK."

"You drove directly home?" Pfeifer verified.

"Yes."

"Can you describe the man?" Roberts asked.

"He had on a dark colored uniform and on the upper sleeve it had a cloth emblem like a Girl Scout badge. Only this one was purple with yellow-gold stitched trim that said Bureau of Police across the top and spelled out "Portland" in gold letters on the bottom," she said.

Pfeifer stopped taking notes and fought back a smile.

"The words would have been easier to read in caps and lower case letters," Laura continued. "He had some sort of cord going up the front of his uniform shirt that was attached to a black gadget he was talking into. A black baseball cap. . . Oh," she said, remembering another detail. "And a gun on his belt."

"Great. Can you also describe the *suspect*?" Roberts asked.

"Oh, was *that* what you meant?" Laura asked. "The robber was five foot nine or ten, wearing a black hoodie and jeans. They were Levis with a leather stitch-on label and they were tight across his butt." She paused then added that the armed man wore running shoes with a Nike swoosh. "They were untied and the laces were muddy."

"Why would you remember that?" Roberts asked.

"I was on the floor," she reminded him.

"Hair color?"

"Probably bloody after he hit that tile floor," she answered.

"Eyes?"

"Two," she said. "I mean clear blue-grey. Both of them."

Detective Roberts' sigh was more exaggerated this time. He got up and walked over to look out the kitchen window.

Laura used the break in questioning to sip her vanilla tea. "Can *I* ask a question?" she inquired. She didn't wait for an answer. "Was that a shot I heard? Is everyone OK?"

"That was the bank guard's gun," Pfeifer said. "He panicked and shot through his shoe."

"This just gets better and better," Esther said quietly.

When Leonard Roberts turned to face Laura again, he changed tactics. "Back to the officer who wouldn't admit you to the crime scene," he said. "A crime scene, by the way, which you should never have left. . ."

"Right," Laura said.

"In case we want to talk to the officer on duty, what else do you remember about *him*?"

"He had a name badge pinned on his shirt that said A. Harrison."

Detective Pfeifer smirked, but continued taking notes quietly. Laura remembered that half grin from the time she had spent with Chris Pfeifer when he was investigating her husband's death.

After Laura described everything she had seen or heard at the bank for a second time, Roberts asked her to write down her recollections "for the record." He told her to report in detail about the robber's appearance and behavior from the time the suspect backed away from the teller's window until he was knocked unconscious.

"May I ask something?" Esther said.

Roberts nodded.

"If you have the suspect in custody, why can't one of you look between the bars to get his description?"

This time Pfeifer laughed out loud. "We could, Mrs. Graham," he said, "but if the case goes to court, we need to know that Laura could identify him. In this case he'll probably take a plea anyway, but we still have to build our case to justify the arrest."

"Makes sense," Esther said.

Roberts turned toward Laura. "You can drop your statement by the police bureau any time tomorrow," he told her. "One other thing," he added. "*Why* would you remember the color and the letters on the officer's sleeve patch?"

"The intensity of the two hues clashed," she said. "Gold and purple can be very dramatic together, in primrose gardens. But you have to watch the intensity."

"Right," Roberts said. "We'll have someone get right on that."

There were no further questions.

"Afraid to make a decorating mistake? Choose cream furniture and add a colorful area rug and matching solid color pillows."

3

Russell Graham was late hearing about the bank robbery.

He slapped together a ham and cheese sandwich on sourdough bread, called it dinner, and moved into his office at Graham Construction. He flipped on the small TV and turned to the Portland news.

There was a fuzzy image of Laura Howard, staring at him from the screen. He listened as the excitable local newscaster reported that the police hoped to find and interview "this brave woman who helped halt a bank robbery earlier today."

The photograph was from footage from the security camera at the bank, the newsman reported.

It sounded to Russ like Laura had walked out of the bank under her own power. That thought was consoling.

He reached in his pocket for his phone to call Esther Graham.

"Aunt Esther, do you have your TV on? Are you watching KGW News?" he asked.

"Why do you ask?"

"Esther, it's a simple question. Did you see a photo of Laura on tonight's TV news?"

"That's old news," she said.

"And?" he prompted.

"Laura wanted to tell you about it herself," Esther said. "The TV news is behind the times. I was with her when the detectives arrived at her house a couple of hours after the robbery to interview her. Detective Pfeifer recognized her right off."

"Of course he did," Russ said. Pfeifer was an OK guy, Russ was willing to admit, but he wished the cop would keep his distance from Laura.

"She's one gutsy lady," Esther added with pride.

"Was she hurt? Tell me she hasn't been arrested."

"Yes and no," Esther said.

She heard Russ take a deep breath.

"Wait," she said. "That's the other way around. Or is it? *No* they didn't arrest her. And *yes* she's OK. Laura was the bystander, not the perp."

Aunt Esther had picked up just enough police jargon to be dangerous, he thought. "And, you both held this information from me all day?"

"She wanted to tell you herself," Esther repeated.

"She'll have her chance. I'm headed up to her place now."

"Don't upset her," Esther said. "She's had a terrible day. There were a lot of people in and out. She needs her rest."

"She needs her damned head examined," he said and disconnected.

Russ put the cell phone in his pocket. He allowed himself five minutes to calm down and think back on the events in Laura's life. During the few years he'd known her, Laura had moved from one catastrophe to the next. He considered it his job to keep her safe, and he was failing at that. They'd dated for several months a year or so ago, but they'd both backed away from a commitment. The spark was still there, but it never seemed the appropriate time to fan the flames.

"Hammer and I are coming up the block," he said without introduction when Laura answered her phone.

"Russ, it's late and I'm exhausted. I had a wild day."

"So I heard," he said. "I won't stay long."

"It's not necessary," she said, but she hoped he'd come.

"We'll be there in three minutes."

Laura carried Louise upstairs and closed him in the guest bedroom. The two animals were not always civil, and she didn't want to referee a pet spat tonight.

She unlocked the front door when she heard Russ' familiar knock and heard him call her name. He stepped inside and held out his arms and she moved forward a step and accepted his warm embrace. She let the tears she had been fighting all evening fall and tried to absorb some of his strength.

"Sorry," she said. "I'm a wimp."

"You're not a wimp. You could have been killed this morning."

"So they tell me," she said. "What scares me is that I didn't worry about that at the time. It's like my fight or flight meter was on the blink."

"I've never been sure you have one."

She ignored the comment. "The bank robbery only took five to ten minutes, but it's consumed my whole day," she said.

"I've got you. You're safe now."

"I keep thinking of the robber staring through me after he shoved that woman. She could have broken a hip . . .'

"And you?"

"He could have shot me," she said simply. "I could have been killed and I never would have seen you and Louise again."

"Weird. That was my first thought. Well, not the part about Louise," he confessed. "When I heard about the robbery, I went from mad to glad in ten seconds."

"You always were a fast mover," she said. "Could you and Hammer use a snack?"

"I think we could all use a drink," he said.

"I better not," she said. "Remember me? One drink and I lose any common sense I have left."

Laura had skipped her scheduled stop at the grocery store after the experience at the bank. She and Russ now scavenged through the near-empty refrigerator and pantry. They passed on white wine and thin Oreo cookies. When they didn't find any soft drinks, they opted for the wine after all, along with some salted crackers and stale pretzels.

"Remember this menu, Ms. Catastrophe," he said as he lifted a cracker to her mouth. "It and a good hug seem to have a soothing effect on you."

"I'm glad you came."

"Me too," he said. "Would you be more at ease sleeping downstairs tonight? Hammer and I could stay until you fall asleep."

"Louise would object," Laura said.

"I'll open the upstairs door for the cat before we leave. I owe that cat an apology for my earlier remark."

He handed Laura two soft print pillows from the chair that sat near the fireplace. Laura curled up on the couch, put the warm pillows between her arm and her head and closed her eyes. Russ covered her with a wool afghan from the back of the couch. She doubted she could go to sleep if she tried. Particularly with Russ watching her.

Russ and the dog remained still while her breathing grew shallow and she drifted off to sleep. He leaned down and kissed her on the cheek and she stirred slightly. He kept his promise to release Louise from upstairs, set the security alarm system, then stepped out the door with Hammer at his heels, and walked back home.

"We could have lost her," he told Hammer.

MAN AND DOG were up early the next morning. Neither had slept much during the night.

Russ had promised Laura last fall that he'd tend to the maintenance on the rain gutters at The Harrington. If he was going to be awake all night worrying about the woman, he might as well use that nervous energy and make good on his earlier offer to complete some simple maintenance.

"I never did understand what you think is wrong with the gutters," Laura said as she inspected the edge of the roof.

"They're supposed to channel the water from the lowest points on the roof to the downspouts," he said. "The ones across your front porch don't have a clear understanding of their job description."

"Right," she said vaguely.

She had noticed before that there was no wasted motion when Russ worked. He reached up to secure the gutter and she could see his muscular chest and upper arms through the worn shirt material.

"I'm freezing and you're wearing a T-shirt," she pointed out.

"I'm working and you're supervising. Our usual division of labor," he teased.

The skin crinkled around his blue eyes when he smiled. She'd noticed that the first day she met the man. If he went too long between haircuts, his dark hair curled in the back and peeked sexily around his ears.

She had mentioned the curls to him once, adding that he looked rugged enough to moonlight as an advertising model for Home Depot newspaper circulars. He'd scoffed at the idea and worked on the other side of the house from her for the rest of that afternoon. Apparently those with Y chromosomes didn't view that comment as a compliment.

"Poof-style ottomans are a short-lived fad. Here today, gone today. Poof!"

4

The snowflakes floated past Laura's kitchen window. It was a beautiful sight, she thought, as she watched the snow collecting quickly on the sloped front lawn at The Harrington. The snowstorm was also a reminder of why the construction company chose these months to close down.

Esther had invited Laura and Russ to have dinner at her place tonight and to review the company accounts before the new building season started. Laura admitted that high finance wasn't her specialty, but knew that the other two would take care of the business details while she concentrated on the artistic side of the partnership at Graham Construction. She'd never work any place again where she had this much freedom in interior design, she thought.

It wasn't that she lacked the smarts and know-how to manage the books. Reviewing the books bored her. She let the other two balance the dollar figures.

She felt awkward when she walked into Esther's apartment. Russ and Hammer were already there. The occasion brought back memories of when Laura and Russ were dating and routinely arrived there as a couple when Esther entertained. She recalled a particularly enjoyable Christmas Eve dinner Russ and she had shared with Esther two or three years ago. She wondered if Russ ever thought about those times.

She relaxed some when Esther served the warm baked shepherd's pie along with a green salad and homemade honey rolls. No one in her right mind would turn down a dinner invitation here, Laura thought.

After clearing the dishes from the main course, Esther reached toward the refrigerator to retrieve her infamous rum-spiked almond cheesecake. While Laura admired the dessert, Russ left to retrieve the financial records they planned to review. It was less than a five-minute walk to and from his office.

"If my watch moves to minute seven, I'm cutting the cake," Laura warned him.

"I think she means it," Esther said.

The cake was of more interest to Laura than the upcoming bookkeeping session. Hammer agreed and wedged himself next to her to be ready in case any crumbs dropped his way.

Laura couldn't help noticing how handsome Russ looked when he returned from his house with snowflakes resting on his dark hair and the shoulders of his navy blue fleece. He'd stomped the snow off his boots before crossing the threshold.

"It's coming down hard and fast out there," he said. "We must have five or six inches of snow already."

"Get in here where it's warm," Esther ordered.

"Have you checked the TV weather channel?" he asked.

Esther had once gloried in working the 8 p.m. to 6 a.m. shift in the Emergency Room at a large Seattle hospital. She had completely embraced the slower pace of semi-retirement now. She could still go at ER speed when it was called for, but she had also learned to relax. She seldom thought about her former job tending to drop-in callers in the ER. Those midnight recipients of knife and gunshot wounds, the victims of automobile accidents, and the surprise deliveries for the next U.S. Census Bureau count were no longer her responsibility.

Russ crossed the small living room space and picked up the remote control for Esther's sixteen-inch television set. The wind rattled against the windows, announcing its own forecast of increasing snow and continued high winds.

"I don't think I've seen snow collect this fast in this part of town before. Imagine how much snow must have fallen in the hills," he said.

Portlanders who lived at the higher elevations routinely dealt with slippery downhill commutes to work in winter. And, it wasn't unusual to find school-age children checking home computers and early morning television broadcasts to see if the school district had declared a "snow day," canceling classes due to concerns for safety on the school bus routes and walkways.

Esther reached down and gave Hammer a rub. "This is what winter's like in Kansas, Toto," she told the dog.

Russ was intent on getting an official weather forecast from the television screen before the electricity failed. He punched the remote control and found a local TV channel. The station had interrupted scheduled programming to broadcast news of a predicted record-setting snow storm that was "sweeping across Oregon and portions of Idaho before heading east."

While the three of them had been enjoying a quiet dinner, the snow had been falling steadily and had already snarled traffic lanes on Interstate 5, the main traffic artery through the state. There were also reports of multiple vehicle accidents involving semi-trucks and triple-trailer rigs that had jack-knifed on the I-5 bridges.

"This is going to be a nasty one," Esther said. "Are you two going to be able to get back down that outside staircase?"

"If we take off right now, we can make it back home safely," Russ said.

Laura glanced longingly at the unserved cheesecake.

The wind buffeted Esther's small upstairs quarters again and Hammer whined. The lights flicked off and on and then off again. Esther dug in a kitchen drawer below the counter and produced a flashlight.

"Be prepared," she said.

"Well, sort of," Russ countered. "Temperatures are going to drop quickly tonight. And, the only spot where we have a generator to keep the lights and heat on at the same time is across the parking area at my place."

The former owner of the house now used for Graham Construction headquarters had placed a generator in the basement when the whole country was preparing for Y2K in the year 2000.

"If we want the big three—hot water, heat, and light—Hammer and I suggest you both spend the night with us."

Could this evening get any more awkward, Laura wondered. "Small problem," she said aloud. "Louise."

"He's welcome to come," Russ said.

RUSS HELD LAURA'S elbow tightly to keep her upright as her leather-soled shoes slid on alternate steps while they walked up the block to The Harrington. Once inside, she gathered warm clothing, some perishable food from the refrigerator, a couple of books, and a winter coat. At the last minute, she circled back to grab her hairdryer.

"We've got time for you to find some boots, too," Russ said.

Russ corralled an irate Louise in a pet carrier to take him back to their emergency quarters. He added a bag of dry cat food on top of Laura's supplies and they headed back outside. Russ used one hand to hold the cat transport cage and the other one to steady Laura on the icy surface.

He had helped Esther across the parking area fifteen minutes earlier. When he and Laura returned, Esther had candles lit and the fireplace kindling in place at Graham Construction.

"This could be quite cozy for a few days," she said. "I'll cut that cake."

The cat spat and snarled from his carrier. Hammer barked and rushed past, knocking Laura into the sofa. Laura spilled the dry cat nibbles from the open bag and was righting herself when Hammer stormed back into the room to clean up the surprise snack.

Fifteen minutes later, Louise was quarantined in the small bathroom and all cautioned not to let her out when they were coming and going from the room.

"Pray for a short storm," Russ said quietly.

"Snow white decor is very striking—if you're willing to spend 23 hours a day cleaning."

5

Laura carefully made her way down the front walk the next morning to retrieve her gloves from (where else?) the glove compartment of her truck. Russ called to her from the side yard.

"How about a snowball fight?"

"No thanks," she called back. "That's so juvenile."

She walked behind the truck and around to the passenger side to retrieve her gloves. She slid back out as she put the gloves on. She tried to stay out of view as she reached across the tailgate to retrieve some snow that had collected in the bed of the truck.

When she had packed three small, firm snowballs in her left hand and balanced one in her right hand, she called out to Russ.

"Changed my mind," she yelled as her first snowball hit splat against the back of his jacket.

She was able to fire off two more snowballs before he came around the back of the truck and chased her into the side yard where the snowball fight started in earnest. The first thing he noticed was that her aim was pretty darn good.

"You ever play any baseball?" he called as he returned fire.

"Nope."

"You're sure?" he asked.

"I was second baseman for a girls' Ponytail Softball League team in high school."

"I can tell," he called back as another snowball whizzed by his ear. It was the first one of hers that had missed. Maybe the answer was to distract the enemy, he thought.

"You're aim's right on for someone who throws like a girl," he yelled as he took two long steps forward, shortening the distance between them.

"I'll show you 'girl,'" she said as she bent down to mold another snowball.

Russ used the pause to move even closer while still holding a handful of snow in both hands. When she hurled the next snowball, he closed the gap between them and cleaned her face gently with the powdery snow in his hands.

"No fair," she yelled, but they were both laughing too hard to keep their balance.

She wondered later if the elderly neighbors across the street had seen the two of them rolling in the snow together. She still hadn't figured out how they went from a fight in the snow to that warm embrace and kiss. It was definitely mutual combat, she thought. She realized how much she had missed those kisses these past months.

Russ returned to the house first and was greeted by an inquiring Esther.

"You two get hurt when you fell out there?" she asked.

"Don't think so."

"Just wondering if we need more liability insurance on the business," she said.

"No. I think our existing coverage is just fine. But thanks for asking."

ONE OUT OF THREE cell phones was in working order at Graham Construction.

Esther often forgot to recharge hers. Laura couldn't find her power cord, but knew she had packed the device when she and Russ gathered up her things two nights before. She accused Louise of hiding it.

Russ had always thought of his house as "of ample size." It had plenty of space for both a residence and a business. It didn't take long, though, before he grew irritable from sharing the space with four extra beings (if you counted the animals, and he did). Laura kept closing herself in her office with the cat, leaving him to deal with Aunt Esther.

He found being under the same roof with Laura twenty-four hours a day frustrating. He was on edge with Aunt Esther there observing their every move. He doubted his proposed snowball fight would go down in the Guinness Book of Records list of smooth romantic moves, but it was a start. He'd initiated a couple of quick goodnight hugs as he and Laura passed in the hallway, but, otherwise, there was no gain in being locked inside together, he thought.

If Esther wasn't messing up the kitchen preparing high fat snacks that none of them needed while residing in a no-exercise zone, she was huffing out the notes to *"Oh, Susannah"* on the harmonica.

She'd had only five minutes to gather necessities, Russ recalled. Who grabs a harmonica?

He had suggested they all stay together for the women's safety, but, after he'd been locked inside with them for a few days, he knew Aunt Esther could probably annoy any intruder to death. The woman was her own self defense team, armed with the harmonica.

There was plenty of dry firewood stacked in the basement and plenty of time. Maybe Esther would turn in early tonight and he and Laura could sit up late in front of the fireplace, he thought.

EACH OF THEM heard the ring tone, but realized quickly that only Russ had an operating phone. The caller was Ernest Gallo asking how Russ and his co-workers were faring in the storm. Ernie Gallo had been hired as the tile man for the Street of Dreams project and had stayed on payroll after the completion of that project. Ernie and Esther Graham were also keeping company, as they said in their day.

Ernie reported that TV announcers were now saying it might be an additional day or two before all snow was plowed from the less-traveled streets in Portland. He offered to drive his Jeep to the grocery store and deliver supplies for the three adults and two pets sharing Russ' home.

"Please, take me with you," Russ pleaded quietly.

"That bad, huh?" Ernie asked.

"You can't imagine," Russ said, thinking the phrase was safe to use in case the conversation was overheard. "Tense. Really tense," he added.

"It can't be *that* bad."

"You've no idea."

Ernie heard strains of harmonica music in the background. "Is that '*Nobody Knows the Trouble I've Seen?*'" he asked.

"I told you. You need to bail me out of here."

THE JEEP ARRIVED in front of Graham Construction later in the day and Russ made his way carefully down the front walkway he had shoveled the day before. The snow was gone, but ice had formed again on the sidewalks late last night when freezing rain fell.

He pulled himself into the passenger side of the Jeep and instructed Ernie to "hit it." Ernie pulled out slowly, heeding the weather and ignoring Russ' instructions.

"I'd think this would be an ideal set up for you," Ernie said.

"You'd think wrong."

"Aren't you the guy who told me over a beer last week that you wanted to seal the deal? That you were thinking of asking Laura to marry you?"

"This is definitely not the time," Russ said. "We've sneaked in a couple of goodnight kisses, but with Aunt Esther there it's like having a third roommate in an eight by eight dorm room.'"

"A woman like Laura only comes along once in a lifetime," Ernie responded.

"You're singing to the choir."

"When purchasing appliances, keep in mind that stainless steel and white fridges keep beer equally cold."

6

The last of the snow melted and the sidewalks were clear of ice by late the next afternoon. The lawns were left muddy and battered where heavy boots had crossed. There was also telling evidence of a snowball fight and ground attack on the side yard at Graham Construction.

Russ helped Esther carry her few belongings back up the stairs to her apartment.

"Did you remember to pack the harmonica?" he asked for the third time.

Esther raised an eyebrow. "You find out who the true music connoisseurs are when you're trapped inside for a few days," she told him. "You didn't hear that dog of yours complaining did you?"

"No, but I suspect I know which one of the inmates kept slipping him dog treats." Esther and Hammer both tried to look innocent.

LAURA TOOK two trips up and down the block to move her things back into The Harrington. She took time on the first trip home to check that the roof hadn't developed any leaks during the storm. It was a tip she had learned from Russ. It was better to inspect for water directly after a storm when fresh damage hadn't had time to dry than to feel the drips on your head during the next downpour.

Russ and Hammer accompanied her as far as the living room on the second trip. She dumped her belongings there, planning to distribute them about the house later.

The house smelled musty from being closed up for a few days. She reminded herself to pick up a spring bouquet at the market when she stopped there to restock the refrigerator.

WHILE SHE'D BEEN encamped at Graham Construction, Laura had worried about what weather-related events might be going on at The Harrington. Leaking roof? Frozen pipes? Run-off water seeping into the basement?

It never crossed her mind that someone—an unauthorized person, as the police would say—would enter her home.

It looked that way now, though.

And, how would I know that they aren't still there, she wondered. Then she remembered that Hammer had come inside with Russ. She knew the dog would have barked himself silly if a stranger had been inside.

Laura was certain all the exterior doors had been locked. But, maybe not. She'd left in a hurry.

Now she walked slowly toward the kitchen counter where someone had placed a yellow lined piece of paper. The corner of the note was weighted down by the edge of the flour canister. How did that happen? And, what did the message mean?

WE KNOW WHO YOU ARE

AND WE KNOW WHAT YOU DID

The note was obviously meant to be creepy, she thought. And, the writer had succeeded on the creep factor. Her first thought was to phone Russ, but she knew he'd overreact.

Did she know anyone who would consider this funny?

The press had gotten hold of her photo and identification after the bank robbery, but had yielded to the police request that her address not be released. Would that have been enough to keep someone from using one of the hundreds of online sites available to track down people? Laura Howard believed in the first amendment, free press and all. But, perhaps not so much when it involved her own safety, she thought

She calmed when she remembered the bank robber was still locked up downtown.

Maybe the message wasn't tied to the bank robbery and her role in disabling the robber. If someone had foiled my attempt to rob a bank, she thought, I'd do something more sophisticated than this to get back at him.

"Unless the note writer wasn't very bright," she said to Louise.

Maybe the note wasn't about the robbery? Had she done something else "noteworthy" that she couldn't recall?

It couldn't have been that dire if I can't remember it, she thought.

Maybe one of the straight-laced elderly neighbors had witnessed Russ and her romping and rolling in the snow? Was the neighbor offended by that lengthy warm kiss? What was the problem? She and Russ were of legal age. Even if they had been acting like fifteen year olds let loose on a high school snow day. . .

She took a deep breath to calm herself. It didn't work.

She wandered from room to room again, checking that every door and window was locked. Had she been careless enough to leave the doors unlocked? Could neighborhood teens have found the house open and decided to prank her with the note. Was it a sign of paranoia that she suspected all of her neighbors? She had to get a grip.

No matter who the note was from, it made Laura uneasy and caused her to mentally relive the bank robbery for the next few hours.

She forced herself to believe this was simple teenage mischief. She wadded up the note and threw it in the fireplace.

No note. No problem.

"Silk flowers last forever, but sometimes mercy killing is in order."

7

"Detective Division. Roberts here."

"This is Laura. Laura Howard," she said into the phone. "You told me to call you if I thought of anything else about the bank robbery."

"Of course," Detective Roberts said.

"I'm not sure if it's important, but I remembered some stuff."

"There's no way I can tell if it's pertinent to the case until you come to the police station and report what you've now remembered."

Laura sensed some impatience in his voice.

"On second thought," he added, "why don't I stop by your place this afternoon while I'm out your way on another case?"

"Do you think the two cases are related?" she asked.

"Not unless you're going to tell me that you're the person who has been blithely streaking nude through the neighborhoods ten to twelve blocks south of your place?"

"In the middle of winter?" she asked.

"Nude nut cases don't carry calendars," Roberts said. "No pockets." He tried not to chuckle at his own joke. "I'll stop by at 4:30 p.m. Before then, take some time to organize your thoughts and maybe even jot some things down so you won't forget what you called to tell me," he said and hung up.

Laura was insulted. She understood the man was overworked, but did he think she'd call him and then forget three hours later what she had to report? She was used to Detective Chris Pfeifer's low key approach and protective manner. She realized, rather sheepishly, that most women weren't on first name basis with even one detective.

MAYBE THE MAN has a point," Russ said when Laura described the detective's retort. "Your life has been full of chaos since he's known you. Now add one bank robbery to the list."

Laura opened her mouth to protest.

"Just saying," Russ added.

"For the record, I don't call 911 for cheap thrills. Sometimes, late at night, I picture a peaceful, grown-up life out on a farm in the middle of Kansas . . ."

"Kansas? What is it with you and Esther and Kansas?"

"I don't know. Kansas, Nebraska, Iowa. Some flat state out there that has warm, billowing breezes and farm houses where I could cook fresh vegetables and hang laundry outside to dry without checking first to make sure there's not a stalker lurking behind the barn."

"This is a whole new side of you," he said.

"It's not where I want to live. It's a day dream I pull up to calm myself when things start to overwhelm me."

"Tornados, drought years, ruined crops, farm loans, weathered dry skin," he listed.

"Russ, forget Kansas already. I'm talking about a state of mind not an actual place."

"Can you call me to remind me when Roberts is due to arrive?" Russ asked. "I want to hear this interview."

THE DETECTIVE was late. Laura had phoned Russ five minutes before Roberts' expected arrival to remind him of the appointment. When Russ arrived, she poured a mug of coffee for him and she was now aimlessly swishing a tea bag through a cup of hot water for herself as they listened for the police car to pull up in front of The Harrington.   The rational side of her brain understood that the detective had a complex job and schedule. The impatient part of her personality began to second guess having called him earlier. Besides, she was hungry. All she'd had to eat today was a bagel and a cup of tea.

"What are you thinking?" Russ asked.

"Two residents starve to death waiting for northwest cop . . ." scrolled through the imaginary CNN scan in her head.

"Nothing much," she said aloud, then corrected herself. "I'm thinking 'let the guy solve his own darn case.'"

"And?"

"I did my part when I helped knock out the robber. Have we even heard the suspect's name?" she asked.

Russ didn't have time to reply before he heard the detective at the door. He showed the weary-looking man to an upholstered chair in the living room. Laura sat on the sofa across from him with her notepad on the small glass table top between them. She didn't plan to actually take notes, but she wanted the detective think that she might.

Russ poured a mug of coffee for Roberts without asking the man his preference of tea or coffee. He reminded himself that his purpose here was to shelter Laura from the abrasive cop, not to serve as barista.

"Ms. Howard," the detective said, "I'm interested to hear what you remembered about the bank robbery you witnessed." He took a careful sip of the hot coffee. "We're wrapping up our investigation now, but it's never too late to hear any information that might be relevant."

There was an awkward pause while Laura weighed whether the information she wanted to report would meet the detective's standards of relevance.

Roberts propped the small laptop computer he had carried in against a book on the glass table top. He appeared ready to write down what she had to tell him. "Shoot," he said.

Laura opened her mouth to make a snappy comeback, but Russ spoke first. "Tell the man what you remembered."

"You'll recall that I left to take something to my truck then couldn't get back into the bank?" she asked.

"Yes. And, I thought we clarified for you that you should not have left the scene."

"You were very clear," she said to Roberts.

"And?"

"And, late last night, I remembered something that happened when I walked back to my truck that day," she said. "I almost got hit by a car that came squealing around the corner and cutting in and out of traffic. At the time I wondered if he was trying to leave the scene or just driving like a jerk."

"That's interesting," the detective said, perking up for the first time since he arrived. "We've assumed so far that the perpetrator was on foot and working solo."

"Was he?" Laura asked.

"I'm not sure we've substantiated that. What do you recall about the vehicle you saw?"

"It skidded around the corner at the same time I heard police sirens approaching," she said. "I remember that because I wondered at the time whether the cops were chasing him or coming to the bank."

"Can you describe the car?"

"It was a Scion."

The detective looked doubtful.

"An older black Scion with a damaged leather bra across the front."

"A *Scion?*"

"Correct. What's wrong with a Scion?" Laura asked defensively.

"Nothing's wrong with a Scion per se," he said. "But, it's not the sort of thing someone remembers days after the fact." He hesitated. "People remember Honda Civics or compact Fords or Chevys. In the history of police reports I can't recall a single speeding Scion."

"Laura's mind doesn't work like others," Russ offered.

"You're not helping," she said and glared at him.

"Right. Right," Roberts said. "Is there anything else you can tell me about the car?"

"It was pretty beat up. Body damage on the front right fender and the passenger door was either coated in flat black paint or primer. It was a poor match."

"I see," the detective said as her wrote. "Anything else?"

"Nope," she said.

"How are you doing since the robbery," he asked pointedly.

"I'm fine as long as you guys don't release the bank robber."

"He'll be with us down at the jail for some time yet."

"Great. How's his head?"

"He's fine," Roberts said. "How are *you* doing, Ms. Howard, after your experience at the bank?"

"My life's pretty much back to normal."

Russ coughed.

"Good. Good," Roberts repeated. "Of course I can't tell at the moment whether or not this information is related to the robbery, but I'll take it back to the team working the case and see if we need to reconsider whether we had a one or two-man job at that bank."

There was another pause before the detective spoke again. "Sometimes that sort of event can leave witnesses shaken for an extended time," he said. "Some seek professional counseling."

Laura bristled.

"Thanks for coming," Russ said as he showed the man to the door.

Laura heard the door latch catch. "How do you spell 'condescending?'" she asked.

"I didn't pick up on that," Russ lied. "Maybe a tad patronizing."

"*A tad?* Should I have called him in the first place?"

"Of course you should have called. If there was a second guy involved in the bank job, he's still out there. And he may think you can identify him."

"Now, there's a happy thought," she said. "That hadn't crossed my mind."

"Well, it needs to," Russ said. "There's too much crap going on in the world to discount anything or anyone."

"I want to thank you for those encouraging words," she said. "If I need help again, I'll ask for Pfeifer. He gives me the same advice, but in a kinder, gentler way. When he leaves, I feel protected."

Those were not the words Russ wanted to hear.

AN HOUR AFTER Detective Roberts left, Laura remembered that she had failed to mention the scribbled note she had found at The Harrington. She decided it probably wasn't important enough to call the detective back. She'd try to remember it if she saw him again.

She'd also forgotten to ask for the suspect's name, but she thought she could get that online on the website of *The Oregonian.*

"A farm table with hard benches, though charming, guarantees guests won't tarry."

8

"Do you have plans for this afternoon?" Russ asked Laura on Saturday morning. "Our down time is slipping away. And I want you to see what I've accomplished while you and the Cat From Hell have been sitting by the fireplace warming your toes and sharpening your claws."

"We're offended," she said. "The gentle Louise and I have been checking out new color combinations for Graham Construction's next home. It looks like coral is back as an accent color, shown against beige, or 'greige' as designers are calling it this year."

"Greige?" Russ asked.

"Dirty beige to you."

"Why don't you take a breather and drive out west of town with me. There's something I want to show you," he said. "That was *you* singular," he added.

"My sweet Louise isn't welcome?"

"If letting that cat loose in a truck cab isn't against the motor vehicle code, it should be."

"Shhh. He'll hear you."

RUSS PURCHASED the plot of land outside city limits before Laura joined the construction company. She knew he'd been hassling with the county to get permission to build a weekend place there. Every time he thought he was one step closer to getting the "go ahead," the inspector would throw another requirement into the mix.

"Have you conquered the county code enforcers?" she asked as he pulled up to the site. It truly was a beautiful piece of land during every season of the year, Laura thought.

"I may have beaten them at their own game," he said. "Hop out and I'll show you the new plan."

Laura saw the same bare land as the last time they'd toured the site. True, that had been during the summer when the trees were leafed out and shading the ground. Otherwise, not much appeared to have changed.

"As far as the folks at the building department go," he said, "I've adopted a new philosophy. If you can't beat 'em . . ."

"This doesn't sound you," she said.

". . . join 'em," he finished.

"I thought you were a rules and 'regs' guy."

"I'm joining the national tiny house movement," he announced. "The rumor is that, as long as the dwelling's on wheels, it doesn't need a permit."

"That sounds too good to be true."

"I'm going to check it out tomorrow afternoon. For now, allow me show you what I plan on building," he said. "We're talking *tiny* house."

"You're not kidding me?" she asked. "You know I love those little places."

Laura had been intrigued for the last two years by the tiny houses with minimal footprints that were popping up throughout the state. She'd shown Russ two different magazine articles describing the small, efficient structures. Each of the write-ups included photos of the modern-day pioneers who were leading the way in the tiny house movement in Oregon. She wasn't aware until now, though, that Russ had actually read those stories.

At the time she'd clipped the articles, she'd been hoping Russ would ask her to marry him and they could live in one of those miniature dwellings. Together.

"I'm hoping you'll help me select a plan to build a tiny house out here where we can hide out from the craziness of work once in a while."

"Wow."

"I know we used to talk about our 'dream house,' but this is a little more realistic. We've got six acres here so I can situate the little place so a full-sized house could be added later by someone with enough energy to tangle with the county officials. That's not me."

He walked off the dimensions of the tiny house he was planning, drawing the boundaries on the muddy ground with the toe of his work boot.

Laura's mind was whirling. He'd said "we," but did he mean the two of them, or Russ and his dog?

Russ stomped out an additional small area.

"What's that?" she asked.

"That could be a sun room, a deck, or maybe a nursery."

"For a very small child," she pointed out. "Or, a very sedate old dog," she said covering her bases. "I'd stick with the sunroom."

"Step into my parlor," he added as he moved his feet into the future living-dining-den area whose boundaries were now also outlined in the mud.

She noticed that he hadn't said "*our* parlor."

"Every space has to serve more than one purpose. This is the total daily living space – plus a tiny kitchen, indoor-outdoor bath in a 'bump out' off the side, and a loft bedroom."

"Is there room for a staircase?"

"Oh, how fast you forget. There's approximately 375 square feet here. The staircase is a ladder."

"Sweet."

He suspected she was the only woman he'd ever meet who would view climbing a ladder to reach the bedroom as "sweet."

And, she suspected he'd never ask her to marry him.

Laura was wandering toward the back portion of the property, an expansive area of natural grasses and a small glen with a glistening pond she could see through the leafless trees this time of year.

She stepped forward to explore the banks of the pond before he could stop her. "I repeat," she called back. "I'd stick with the sunroom. This pond doesn't look safe for a kid."

"Slow down," Russ said. He was trying to keep up as she approached the reed-covered banks of the pond. He reached for her hand. "There's something I want to ask you."

"Isn't this gorgeous with the sun reflecting off the water? You knew the pond was here when you bought the property? And you never told me?"

"Could you stand still a sec?"

He hadn't picked out an engagement ring yet, but maybe it didn't matter. Maybe an impromptu proposal was better, he thought.

"Wait!" she said. "Will this place have a laundry room?"

"Wait?" he repeated.

"Environmentalists will freak if you do laundry in the pond," she said. She stepped closer to the water.

Her left foot slid.

Russ followed and grabbed her hand. When she reached the edge of the pond, she lost traction again and slipped into the shallow pond, pulling Russ in behind her.

"Oops!" she said.

"I wanted today to be memorable."

"This is pretty darn memorable."

"In its own way, I suppose," he said. "Not at all how I planned it, but standing in three feet of icy water won't be easy to forget." He reached for her other hand and turned her to face toward him. "Laura, will you marry me?"

Her surprised response was drowned out by the splash created as she fell backwards into the shallow water.

"Was that a 'yes' or a 'no?'" he asked.

"A 'yes'. Definitely yes," she said between chattering teeth. "But for now, it may have to be a 'yes, but.'"

"Do you suppose we could get back on dry land before you explain that to me?"

They made their way back to the truck cab where Russ wrapped a red plaid Pendleton wool blanket around the two of them and they sealed the proposal with a kiss. She leaned over to kiss him again, but he pulled back.

"No more kisses until you tell me what this 'yes but' business is all about."

"I want it to be the happiest day in our lives when we get married."

"Of course," he said.

"So could you ask me again when all the bank robbery and police stuff dies down? I want to be able to think about only us."

"If that's how it has to be, that's how it has to be," he said and pulled her into his arms.

They returned to Portland late afternoon with what Esther would later describe as Cheshire cat grins on their faces.

"THERE WAS a young woman here this morning asking for you," Esther said to Russ the next day.

"Laura?"

"Wouldn't I have said 'Laura' if that's who she was asking for?"

"A little snippy this morning, are we?" Russ asked.

"No. I just took an instant dislike to this woman. She left a business card for you. Russ. She verified that Laura was the 'woman from the bank robbery,' but said she was here to talk to you about Laura's role at Graham Construction. Anyway, that's what she claimed."

Esther handed Russ a business card from one of the local TV news desks.

"If she's following up on the bank robbery story, why wouldn't she interview Laura?"

"Precisely," Esther responded. "I've got a feeling she'll be back. She was pretty persistent."

"A white picket fence turns even a hovel into a charming cottage."

9

"Hammer," Russ said. "I'm glad you weren't with us over the weekend to watch me make a fool of myself."

The sheepdog continued eating.

"I tried to make good on our resolution, old boy, but I got put on hold."

Russ and Hammer had made a New Year's Eve resolution to include Laura in their future. Russ doubted that his dog understood that plan, but, after three glasses of champagne at home alone on New Year's Eve, he'd thought it reasonable to keep the dog informed.

Russ turned his attention away from Hammer, and glanced out the front window at Graham Construction. He saw Laura's truck moving past.

"Pray she's not headed into a hold up this time," he told the dog. Protecting Laura was a full time job, one that Russ knew he wanted for life.

He pulled down the Roman shade on the living room window and moved toward the kitchen to open a can of baked beans for him and to refill Hammer's food dish. There was nothing to be gained by having a near-stroke every time Laura left the house, he thought. And, it would be stalking to put a tracking device on her truck, he chided himself.

"Plus, we probably wouldn't be able to match the color to her satisfaction," he told the dog.

LAURA WOKE early the next morning but elected to stay in bed nestled under the down comforter. When her cell phone rang, she inched her arm out from under the blanket and reached for it.

"Aunt Esther?" she asked into the phone.

"One and the same," came the response.

"I'm glad you called. Do you have time to talk? And are you alone?"

"Ever since I booted my fourth husband," Esther said. "Your voice sounds strange, are *you* alone?"

"Yes."

"You sound upset," Esther said.

"I am upset. I'm afraid I'm going to end up an old maid with a cat. No insult to Louise here," she added. She described briefly how she had stalled Russ when he asked her to marry him. "And, now he's treating me like a co-worker instead of a girlfriend."

"And you're surprised?" Esther asked. "He got up his nerve to ask and you slam-bashed his male ego."

"Well, maybe. That wasn't my intent."

"Intent be damned," Esther said.

"I didn't think I should make a major decision when I'm so preoccupied with everything that's been coming at me since the bank robbery."

"You're using logic," Esther said. "He was running on testosterone."

"Is there any way to turn this mess around?"

"Let me think on it, dear."

"This needs to stay private," Laura said. "Private with a capital P. In bold face."

"Gotcha."

"I don't want Russ to think I went running down the middle school row of lockers, telling everyone I saw that he asked me to go steady."

"My lips are sealed," Esther said. "Trust me."

LAURA'S CELL PHONE rang again immediately after she disconnected from her call with Esther.

"Have I reached Laura Howard? This is Detective Pfeifer calling from the Portland Police Bureau."

"How would I know that for sure?" Laura asked.

"Good for you! You're getting some street smarts. I'm at the Bureau. Call me right back." He hung up.

"Shall we start again?" she asked when Chris Pfeifer picked up the desk phone at work.

"I was calling to alert you that the suspect we had in custody for the bank robbery is going to be released late this afternoon."

"Why? How?" Laura gasped.

"He had a stack of misdemeanors in his past, several driving infractions, and minor in possession of pot. . ."

"And?"

". . . but no prior felony charges. He hired himself a hotshot attorney who's new in the area. They got the arraignment hearing scheduled for this morning, and he's being released on bail. He'll still come before a judge on the charges. In the meantime, he'll be wearing one of our designer ankle bracelets and we'll know if he leaves his home."

Laura didn't respond.

"Are you still there?"

"I'm here, but I'm not happy."

"These things are frustrating to the police too. For what it's worth, my read after watching the film from the bank security camera was that this guy might have been more strung out than dangerous the day of the robbery."

"He had a gun."

"A replica, it turns out," Pfeifer said.

"Made no difference at the time to those of us on the floor."

"That's true," Pfeifer said. "The guy will be on our radar while he's out," he assured her.

"Does this guy have a name?"

"Didn't we remember to give that to you?" he asked.

"If you did, I've forgotten it."

"That's not very likely. It's John Smith"

RUSSELL GRAHAM planned to tie in a drive past the McDonald's window for lunch with a second stop at Copeland Lumber. He glanced in the truck's rearview mirror to back out and saw a low sports car pulling in behind him.

The driver of the other vehicle hit the horn to draw attention to her presence. Russ thought that was overkill since he couldn't go anywhere until she moved her vehicle. He watched as an attractive young woman unfolded herself from the late model Porsche and walked up to the driver's side of the truck. Russ rolled down the window.

"You must be Russell Graham," she said in as casual a tone as if they'd been standing along the same wall at a cocktail party.

"Could I help you?"

"I'm sure you can," she said sweetly.

"I'm running a little late. Could you please get to the point?"

"Sorry. I'm Candace Galassi," she answered. "From Portland's top-rated TV news station. But, I'm sure you know that already."

Russ didn't recognize the woman. "How can I help you?" he repeated.

"Maybe you could cut the engine on the truck for a start," she said.

Russ turned the key in the ignition. The driveway was immediately quieter.

"I'd like to ask you some questions about your business partner Laura Howard. The woman who may well have inflicted life-threatening injuries on a young man at a local bank."

"What?"

"I'd like to ask you. . ." she started to repeat.

"My hearing is fine. You need to move on so I can drive out to the lumber yard. I didn't witness the bank robbery. And, I definitely don't plan to talk to you about my business partner."

She smiled, looked down, then up again and met his eyes. "And, I think you're sweet for trying to protect Ms. Howard. Maybe we could meet over coffee on a day when you have more time?" she asked. "I'd be happy to change my schedule for you."

"Would you be just as happy to move your car for me? Now?"

She turned on her heel, got in the sports car, and squealed out of the yard.

LAURA HADN'T told Russ yet that the bank robber had posted bail. Pfeifer had explained to her that, while bond was set at $250,000, the guy only had to post ten percent of that.

If the suspect had twenty-five thousand dollars lying around, Laura wondered, why would he rob a bank?

She meant to ask Russ that, but the last two times she'd seen him, he'd been deep in conversation with Esther. She assumed they were talking about Graham Construction finances while she was pondering the amount in the robbery suspect's accounts.

"Overhead kitchen pot racks are for short cooks and head bangers."

10

There was no wind outside, yet Laura thought she heard something scraping against the house. There it was again. This time it sounded like someone tapping against the window in the TV room where she and Louise were sharing a ceramic mug of hot chocolate and watching the last five minutes of "House Hunters" on television.

She walked toward the window, and the sound stopped.

"My imagination," she told the cat.

The next time, they both heard the noise and Louise leaped from the couch and hid under the leather club chair in the corner.

"You're such a wuss," Laura told him while she contemplated whether there was room for two under that chair.

Someone was out there. She was sure of it.

She phoned Russ, but got no answer. Maybe he was at Esther's place. She tried that number next and woke Esther.

"Is there a weapon in the house?" Esther asked when Laura described the problem.

"Of course not."

"So, no gun," Esther confirmed. "Then, pick up your cell phone in one hand and Louise in the other. Go door to door making sure everything's locked. If someone springs out at you, throw the cat at him," she said. "I'm calling the police from here."

"Throw Louise?"

"Louise is your bayonet."

THE POLICE WERE prompt and circled Laura's house on foot before ringing the front door bell.

Laura held Louise wrapped in a sweater so the cat wouldn't slip out the door when she unlocked it to let the officers inside. The men were soaking wet, dripping water from their rainproof ponchos onto the polished hardwood floor in the entryway. For once, Laura didn't care how wet the floor got. She welcomed the protection.

Louise stayed undercover.

Laura didn't recognize either officer. The younger man took the lead.

"What size shoe do you wear?" he asked.

She looked startled at the abrupt question. There had been no introductions, no verification of the right address, no apology for dripping through the living room.

"The size of your shoe?" he repeated.

"We're not even on first name basis. Why do you ask?"

"Ms. Howard. . ."

"Laura," she corrected him.

"Mike," he responded, completing the introductions. "When I made the rounds of your house with a flashlight just now, I found a single footprint from what could have been a large boot in the mud on the south side. That smudged footprint was outside what I see now is your TV room window."

"Large like Bigfoot?" Esther Graham asked as she came through the front door.

"Don't do that," the officer told her. "One of us could have pulled our gun on you."

"Sorry."

"Are you a neighbor?"

"Esther Graham," she said. "Laura's confidante, friend, neighbor and business partner."

"Shoe size?" he asked.

"A dainty size 5," she said without quibble.

He glanced at Laura's pink fuzzy slippers. "And, I can assume that you don't wear a size 13 or 14 either."

"Seven and a half."

"Do you have a yard guy?"

"Just me," Laura said. "What's freaking me out is that the cat and I sit in that room every evening to watch television."

"I have to ask some awkward questions on a call like this," he said. "Are you two fully dressed when you're downstairs?

"I'm sometimes in a heavy bathrobe, but Louise never changes." She hesitated. "Is that bad?" she asked. "Our usual pattern is to go up to bed at the end of the 10 o'clock local news."

"You may have had a Peeping Tom. These guys will often look for several nights and then they'll return and make some sort of noise intentionally so you'll know you're being watched."

"In pouring rain?"

"It worked in our favor tonight. It was wet enough to make mud and capture that print on the ground under the roof overhang. Did you hear anything unusual last night? Earlier this week?"

"I'd have called the police if I did. This gives me the creeps. Do you think somebody's been standing there watching us?"

"*Us?*" he repeated.

"The cat and me." She put Louise down on the floor and he made a run for the staircase.

"Very possibly," the cop said. "There's no way to know how frequently you may have been observed."

"This scares the crap out of me," Esther said.

"You and me both," Laura responded. "The sheers come down tomorrow morning and thick drapes will be hung before dark," she said. "Does this kind of person just look or do I have to worry about him breaking into the house?"

"I'll have patrol circle past here a few times a night for the next ten days. There's no way to tell if we scared him off or if he'll be back."

He handed Laura his business card with a case number written on it, mumbled something about making a report, and he and the other man were out the door. They were gone before Laura realized neither of them had answered her question about whether "peepers" moved on to breaking and entering. Or worse.

Laura and Esther stood in the doorway where they could overhear the cops talking while they walked back to their squad car.

"You want me to send out an alert about Bigfoot?" the older cop asked.

"There's no effen Bigfoot out on a rainy night in Portland."

"I'll take that as a 'no.'"

"Forget the over-sized creature. Send the alert."

"Choose occasional chairs with exposed legs. They're sexy and make the room appear more spacious."

11

Laura knew it was a false sense of security, but she had felt more at ease when the bank robbery suspect was in jail. Now both he and the possible get-away-car driver were loose.

Could either of them be the Peeping Tom? The thought made her skin crawl. It was definitely time to accept Russ' offer to add state-of-the-art locks on all the exterior doors and windows at The Harrington.

She spent the day stitching opaque fabric panels to hang in the downstairs windows. She varied the color of the drapes to match each room's décor, but lined all the curtains with white fabric so the house would look uniform from the outside at night. It was an interior update she'd planned to make anyway, but she hadn't been in any hurry. She felt more urgency now. She'd work until midnight if necessary to make sure no one could see inside The Harrington tonight or any other night.

The monotonous sewing routine calmed her. She could let her mind wander while she sewed. And, as expected, it wandered to Russ' proposal. She wondered if he'd favor moving to The Harrington with her or if he'd ask her to live at Graham Construction.

As much as she'd loved her vintage house, she no longer felt at ease here. Her preference, she realized, would be to live at Graham Construction and spend weekends at the tiny house. She didn't think she'd ever feel completely relaxed at The Harrington again. And, she'd been dying to decorate the Graham Construction house since her first day on the job. Maybe Mr. Peeper was a blessing in disguise, she thought.

Would Russ be a willing accomplice if she wanted to update the living quarters at Graham Construction? The small bedroom there would make an ideal kid's room some day.

She visualized a no-frills and gender neutral décor for a house they would share. Her mind wandered to the time she and Russ had met in the hallways at Graham Construction for late night hugs when they were trapped by the snowstorm.

She daydreamed about the peaceful look of seaside homes featured in decorating magazines. She wouldn't mind adding a touch of the nautical look to Russ' house, but she couldn't overdo it since Portland sat a hundred miles from the Oregon coast.

The draperies were finished by late evening. She wondered later how she had avoided stitching through her fingers while she daydreamed.

"LAURA, ARE you awake?"

"Isn't the answer to that 'I am now?'"

"Sorry to wake you," Russ said into the phone, "but Hammer and I took our morning walk and we're outside the front of your house. Have you looked outside?"

"That would be a 'no,'" she said as she rubbed her eyes and tried to become more fully awake. "I don't usually keep my nose pushed against the downstairs window waiting to see you two manly men walk past." She paused to look at the alarm clock. "At 6:15 in the morning. This had better be good."

"I think you'd better get dressed and come on out to the front yard." He hung up.

Laura climbed out of bed and threw on jeans and a sweatshirt and her black summertime flip flops that she knew wouldn't dissolve if she walked across the dew-covered lawn and down to the sidewalk.

Her toes were already cold.

"This had better be good," she said aloud.

She opened the front door and looked to where Russ and Hammer were standing.

As she walked closer, she saw the evidence of tire treads where a vehicle had driven up and over the curb and smashed into her parkway tree with enough force to snap the trunk. The second set of tire treads looked like the driver had backed up and made another swoop forward to make sure the tree was dead and all the primroses pulverized into the ground.

"You've got to be kidding me," she yelled. 'I've been an awesome Tree Mom. I've nursed that tree to good health for over two years. What idiot would do this to an innocent tree?"

Hammer walked over and sat down on Laura's feet. It instantly warmed her toes but didn't make up for the senseless vandalism.

"I loved that tree," she said quietly. "It was finally thriving and about ready to leaf out for another year."

"You didn't hear anything during the night?" Russ asked. "Nothing woke you?"

"No. Louise and I are super-vigilant after Tuesday's Peeping Tom incident. We turned in about midnight after I'd finished stitching some drapes."

"You need more sleep," he said.

"Thank you, Dr. Graham," she said. "Too bad you're not a tree surgeon."

"It wasn't icy so no motorist unintentionally slid across here. Do we think this was a drunk driver or a deliberate act of vandalism?"

"After everything else that's been going on around here, I'd guess vandalism. And stupidity," she added.

"You should probably report it in case there were other incidents of vandalism in the neighborhood."

"Could you do it for me? I'm afraid if the cops see my name on caller ID again, we'll hear the group groan clear out here."

Russ made the call.

PFEIFER ARRIVED mid-morning to take a report and snap some photos to show Leonard Roberts when he returned to the office.

"I don't often come out on a call like this, but I'm worried about the number of incidents that are stacking up here," he told Russ.

"I've been telling Laura that."

Laura frowned at both of them.

"Is there any on-going feud in your neighborhood?" Pfeifer asked her.

"Of course not."

"Could the three of you ask around and see if any of the neighbors are experiencing any exterior vandalism, either in their yards or on their homes?"

"I can do that part," Esther volunteered as she joined the group.

Pfeifer handed Laura his business card.

"I must have close to a full deck of these now," she said as she reached for yet another Portland Police Bureau business card with a case number scribbled on the back.

Pfeifer admired the woman's spirit. He grinned at her and loped back to his car to take the next call.

RUSS AND ESTHER Graham stepped inside The Harrington to sample some coffee cake Laura had baked while waiting for the police to arrive. Aunt and nephew resumed the line of questioning where Detective Pfeifer left off.

"Did you know a single extortionist, burglar, arsonist, vandal, bank robber or graffiti artist before you married Todd Howard?" Esther asked.

"Of course not."

"How about white collar crime? Have you ever dated anyone who was into credit card fraud? Embezzlement? Cybercrime? Identity theft? Forgery?" Esther asked .

"You left out counterfeiting," Russ said.

"My mistake."

"I'm not sharing my past dating history with you two," Laura told them. "It's not that bad."

"It's that bad," Russ said quietly.

"You two make it sound like I recruit gangsters," Laura protested. "Except for the little trouble we had at the Street of Dreams . . ."

"Three murders and a kidnapping?" Russ asked, verifying Laura's definition of "a little trouble."

". . . my life has been relatively calm," she continued.

"Relatively." Russ repeated. "Until you conked a bank robber!"

"That was the other guy's idea."

"There's no need to be modest. You knocked him out cold."

"Newborns arrive matched to the exact measurements of a lower dresser drawer. Lavishly decorated nurseries are for parents."

12

"Hey, Russ. Ernie here."

Russ was surprised by the call because he knew Ernie wasn't keen on using the telephone when he could drive a few miles and have a conversation in person.

"Anything wrong?"

"I hope not," Ernie said. "Some lady was on my porch just now asking me questions about your business and, particularly, about Laura and her interior design skills?"

"Did you see what she was driving?"

"Laura?"

"No. The lady who arrived on your porch."

"Duh! Of course that's what you meant," Ernie answered. "Looked like the new 911 Carrera Porsche that just came off the line. Ninety thousand dollars plus wheels."

"Beautiful car, you've got to admit." Probably a good thing I didn't throw the truck in reverse and back over it, he thought.

"She claimed she's from some local news show and maybe she is. I didn't recognize her. But, it seemed to me that, if she could find *me* to pester, she could find Laura and talk to her face to face."

"What did you tell her?"

"I lay tile."

Russ chuckled. "Good answer," he said. "Did you get the feeling that she was 'coming on' to you?"

"Laura?"

"Of course not!"

"Let's just say that in my younger days I might have hopped in the side door if this young driver asked me to take a ride with her."

"You didn't get any idea what information she was digging for?"

"I didn't give her time to do any digging."

"Good call," Russ said.

"Do me a favor and don't mention this to Esther," Ernie said.

"Second good call."

MOST OF THE NEIGHBORS weren't awake when Russ pulled up along the curb in front of Vance Denham's house. The two men had been neighbors for half a dozen years, but had talked only twice that Russ recalled. He remembered visiting with Denham once when they were both shoveling the driveways in winter. The rest of the time, they waved when they saw each other and were careful not to back into each other's vehicles as they put their cars in reverse and left their driveways early mornings.

Vance walked around to the driver's side of the truck and got right to the point of why he had hailed Russ.

"You know," he said, "I was one of the neighbors who supported the zoning variance so you could have your construction business in a residential neighborhood," he said.

"I remember that," Russ said, "and I hope we've lived up to our end of the deal by not creating a noise nuisance."

"Absolutely," Vance said. "And it beats having a family with six kids in there, spending their evenings playing ball in the street while I'm trying to catch the game on TV."

Russ thought street ball would have been fun, but he didn't say so. Summertime street games were among his fondest childhood memories.

"So, what's on your mind?"

"Now, you know, I'm not a complainer," the man started.

"Agreed," Russ said.

"But, I'm wondering what you can tell me about your women employees."

"I don't have any women employees," Russ started. "Are you talking about my business partners Esther Graham and Laura Howard?"

"The young one. The one who bought the preacher's place."

"That's Laura Howard," Russ said. "She's an interior decorator when our company's up and running. We've all been on an extended break these past two months while new construction is slow."

"How well do you know the Howard woman?" Denham asked.

Russ avoided answering him directly. "What's your concern?" he asked.

"It's my wife's concern as much as it is mine. There are police cars coming and going over there all hours of the day and night. We wondered for a while if she was running some sort of drug operation, what with all the come and go traffic."

"Laura? Never."

"Yeah. We decided that, too. It's mostly cops pulling up out front lately, not druggies. We can't figure what's going on. All we know is that this was a quiet residential neighborhood before she bought that place. I'm sure you can understand our concern."

Russ started to speak, but was interrupted.

"Don't get me wrong. She keeps that front yard in beautiful shape, what with the flower gardens, parkway tree and all." He hesitated. "She is going to restore that parkway, isn't she?" he asked.

"Let me give you a little history," Russ said. "Laura and her cat live a very quiet life. Lately, though, she's been dealing with vandalism at her place. That's why the police cars are coming and going."

He didn't feel it was his place to give the neighbor details about the bank robbery or a rundown of Laura's life during the last few years. If she wanted to share things, that was her business. Russell Graham knew every neighborhood had a "town crier," but he didn't hold that title on this block.

"That puts a different light on it. Is there anything the neighbors can do to help her?"

"I'm not sure," Russ said. "You might let folks know that the police are patrolling here more regularly at night to see if they can keep vandalism from spreading throughout the area. I've told them down at the Police Bureau this isn't customary on the block."

"Agreed," the neighbor said. "One other thing. We heard sirens the other night. Did those stop out behind her place?"

"Could have."

THREE DAYS LATER every neighbor found a hot pink piece of paper lightly taped to his front door.

Vance Denham and Anthony Gargenzio, two of the senior neighbors, had distributed the pink handbills to invite interested neighbors to a pot luck dinner in the Denhams' open living/dining room to discuss forming a Neighborhood Watch Group. Folks were to meet at 6 p.m. Thursday and bring a "hot dish," salad or dessert.

And their own drink if they wanted something stronger than lemonade. . .

"An open floor plan allows every member of the family to make unreasonable demands on Mom while she's cooking."

13

At first Laura thought the crash she heard was the sound of something falling over on the front porch. Perhaps a potted plant or one of the terra cotta bird statues (Oregon Meadowlarks?) she had balanced on the side railing had fallen.

She was listening for any additional noises when the home alarm siren blasted through the house. The alarm startled her and she hit her head on the bed post.

"Russ and that damn alarm." Laura told Louise. "We've caught a garden pot in the middle of a crime spree."

Russ had insisted that she have the "blaring thing" installed several years ago. This was the first time she had heard it go off since the day the installer tested it. The alarm control panel was located on the inside wall at the bottom of the stairway. She put on her robe and walked downstairs to push the "off" button that was flashing on the panel.

"What happens now?" she wondered aloud, then remembered that someone from the alarm company would be telephoning within seconds.

She swung around the newel post at the bottom of the stairs, turned on the overhead entryway light, and came to a halt.

The living room floor was a mess of shattered glass reflecting in the light and sparkling up from the shiny wood floors. She hoped the original wood flooring hadn't been gouged. In the middle of the glass shards lay what looked like a wadded up newspaper. Then she glanced to the side and saw that the lower half of the front window was broken.

This wasn't caused by flower pots, she thought. They would have fallen onto the porch, not jumped up and flung themselves through a window.

She reached to turn on the lamp on the side table and glanced again at the discarded wad of newspaper. Paper isn't heavy enough to break a window, she thought. She looked again and suspected that something the size of a large rock might be wrapped in the newspaper.

Laura went back upstairs to corral Louise in the guest bedroom. Little paws could pick up glass slivers.

She took time to change from her own soft-soled slippers to tennis shoes. As long as she didn't plan to stomp on the glass those should protect the soles of her feet.

Her cell phone was resting on the night stand where she routinely left it within reach so she could access it in case of an emergency. Like now, she thought. The phone began to chirp, undoubtedly signaling that the night operator at the alarm company was calling.

Laura thought about the shattered window again. There was no way someone could reach from there to unchain the front door or throw the deadbolt. They'd have to be either a contortionist or a great ape. That comforted her. A little. At least the idiot who threw something through the window wasn't lurking inside the house with her.

She picked up the phone.

The night operator at the alarm company verified that Laura wasn't hurt and that no one had entered the dwelling "to the best of your knowledge, dear."

Laura confirmed that.

"I'll be in touch with the police and give them the basic information you've reported to me," the operator told her. "They'll usually have a patrol car circle the neighborhood for a few hours after an incident like this. These aren't always isolated events."

"Thanks."

"They'll give you a call in the morning," the operator added. "First let me verify your street address and contact information."

"No need," Laura said. "The cops know this address by heart."

"WE'VE HANDLED the situation," she explained to Louise. There was no need to call Russ or Esther.

She'd talk to the police in the morning, but she didn't see what good it would do. She hadn't seen or heard a stranger walking past. She assumed one of her friends would have phoned—not thrown—if they wanted to get her attention. She hadn't heard a vehicle. And, perhaps most noteworthy, neither she nor Louise had been alerted by heavy footsteps on the porch.

Laura made the only rational decision a scared interior decorator could make. She decided to remain awake and keep busy until morning. She left the cat locked upstairs and reached for a broom to clean up the mess. She systematically swept the living room floor, moving from there to the utility room wastebasket and back, dumping the contents of the dustpan into the trash can. Sweeping and dumping. Sweeping and dumping. If she hadn't been so angry, she might have appreciated the musical sound made when the shards of glass hit the bottom of the metal waste container. Not tonight.

Laura had picked up some basic knowledge from her contacts with the police through the years. She knew not to touch the crumpled newspaper. She carefully swept around it.

She was still concerned that both she and Louise were in the habit of going barefoot in the house year round. She shifted all of the furniture to one side of the living room, and swept the exposed flooring. She relocated the furniture a second time and swept again. As a final thought, she shifted all the furniture again and applied a light coat of liquid wax diluted with water to the wood floors which gleamed in appreciation.

She systematically worked around the newspaper-wrapped package that sat on the floor in the middle of the room. She didn't think there could be fingerprints on crumpled newspaper, but she didn't want to be scolded when the police arrived.

She sat down to rest and surveyed the room. How long had the furniture been in the same configuration?

By 7 a.m., each piece of furniture rested in its new place. "Perfect," she said to the loveseat now relocated by the front window. "Although you could use a couple of throw pillows," she said aloud.

The next time she walked through the living room she switched the positions of the two occasional chairs that flanked the fireplace and moved the glass coffee table closer to the sofa. "Better."

DETECTIVE CHRIS PFEIFER arrived alone this time. He'd read the incident report when he came into work that morning and offered to "snag that one" since he was familiar with the site.

Laura opened the door for him and he froze in the entryway.

"Stand still," he commanded.

She followed his order.

"Don't move a muscle," he said. "For real. And, where's that monster cat of yours?"

"Upstairs. In a closed room."

"Is he an indoor-outdoor model or a house cat?"

"All weather model," she said. "But, he's always inside at night. Am I allowed to ask why it matters?"

"Did it even cross your mind that the wrapped item only five feet behind us is the exact size of a common explosive device?" he asked.

"Crap."

"That pretty much sums it up."

"So, now what?" she asked.

"Go up and get the cat. Put him in a pillowcase and carry him downstairs."

"You haven't spent a lot of time with Louise, have you?" she asked.

She'd noticed recently that Pfeifer had lost the little boy look he had when she had first met him. Dealing with life and death on a daily basis probably did that to you, she thought.

"Your pet needs to be outside with us and I'm afraid if he sees me in the living room he'll freak and skid right into that thing."

"You do know Louise," she said.

"Once the cat's contained, we all three back out the front door slowly and carefully. Don't close the door behind us," he ordered. "You can take the cat to a neighbor's house, but don't let him loose. We don't want him returning to the house until we figure out what that thing is."

"Got it."

"I'm going to feel dumb as a rock . . ."

". . . if it's a rock," she finished for him.

LAURA WENT first and Pfeifer followed with his forearm under the pillowcase containing the cat.

He ushered her toward the police car. "You and the cat can sit in the front passenger seat while I call and get someone out here."

"Do we need to warn the neighbors?" she asked.

"No, but I'm going to move the car farther up the block," he said. "Even if that thing blows, I don't think it'll take out more than a small part of your house," he said. "The bomb guys en route will know more about it. We'll let them decide whether to evacuate the area."

Laura didn't find that very comforting.

"You can drop the cat off at Mrs. Graham's place if it makes you more comfortable than detaining him in the car."

She noted the police jargon used to describe "detainee" Louise, but didn't comment.

LAURA WAS MISTAKEN if she thought she could pull off Louise's early morning visit at Esther's apartment as a neighborly house call. She gave Esther a news update on the unfolding story at The Harrington before she rejoined Pfeifer.

"The thing could still be a rock. But, we're going to make darned sure before we start playing catch with it," he said.

THE ALL CLEAR came about thirty minutes after the bomb squad entered the house. Pfeifer's "explosive device" turned out to be a common river rock that looked suspiciously like the ones that had lined Laura's front parkway garden.

Pfeifer delivered the news to Laura along with Russ and Esther who had now joined them in front of the house.

"I'd like to tell you it was an over-reaction on my part," the detective said. "And, in truth, I probably wouldn't have reacted that way at any other address in town, but..."

"Are you casting aspersions on The Harrington?"

"You've got to admit that there've been more than the usual number of calls on this stretch of the street," Pfeifer said.

"You sound like the head of our new Neighborhood Watch Group," Esther said.

"And, all's not well, yet," Pfeifer said. "Let's step back inside the house. I want to show you a note that was wrapped inside the newspaper."

"A note? From someone I know?"

"You tell me."

They sat down at the dining room table and Pfeifer handed Laura the note, now encased in a clear plastic evidence bag. Russ stood to read it over her shoulder.

KEEP YOU MOUTH SHUT BICH

"Whoever wrote it isn't highly educated," Laura said.

"He can't spell," Russ pointed out.

"And, he thinks he's starring in a CSI rerun," Esther added.

Each of the letters in the note was cut out of a magazine and pasted to the piece of paper which had been wrapped around the rock and then wrapped with the newspaper.

"Who cares if he can spell?" Laura asked. "He's been within a few feet of my porch in the middle of the night."

"Do you think he pitched the rock from the lawn or from a car going by on the street?" Russ asked.

"Can't tell."

"Be glad the pitch was low and outside. He missed the stained glass window," Esther said.

"Why do you all assume it's a man?" the detective asked.

"Look at the typefaces he chose for the note. A woman would have selected similar styles, colors and weights of type," decorator Laura answered.

"Interesting theory."

Esther was busy examining the newspaper page. "Did you take a close look at this newspaper?" she asked. "The top story's about the bank robbery Laura was involved in."

"For the last time, I was not *involved* in a bank robbery."

ESTHER ALERTED the Neighborhood Watch Group (NWG to members) that "an incident" had occurred. She was among the first to be able to report trouble on the block since their organizational meeting. One of the other members grumbled that Esther had an unfair advantage since she knew "that Howard woman."

Esther filled out the NWG report form and suggested that other members be particularly vigilant for the next few shifts.

"Ebony floors are charming if you vow to give up pets, children, and crumb donuts."

14

The only time Laura felt at ease (pronounced "sane") any more was when she was concentrating on a design proposal. She could become absorbed in the task for two or three hours without thinking about bank robberies, vandalism or home invasions.

She wanted to update the upstairs master bedroom at The Harrington before she and Russ were married.

If we're married, she thought. There had been no further discussion about getting married or where they would live if they did become Mr. and Mrs. Graham. In the tiny house? At Graham Construction? Here, at the house she and Louise called home?

It was time to neutralize the colors in the master bedroom anyway, Laura thought. Careful design choices could make a room appealing for both men and women. If men took the time to notice, she thought.

"If that had been a grenade in the living room," she told Louise, "you and I wouldn't have had a house to redecorate." The cat ignored her and continued his nap in the middle of the bed. "We'll keep this simple so we're not mid-project when the next Graham Construction build gets underway."

By the following weekend, the bedroom had been transformed into a peaceful retreat. She'd wait until she knew if more than she and the cat were going to live there before she hired Ernie to retile the adjoining bath.

The bedroom walls were now coated with soft, warm taupe paint that served as a mellow backdrop for the deep wine, navy and aqua accessories. She selected a round cream sculptured rug that peeked out from each side of the bed and would keep bare feet warm when they first reached the floor in early morning. As a final touch, she artfully tossed a fake fur throw across the end of the bleached wood bed.

Even if Russ never sees the room, I like it, she thought. She threw herself backwards across the bed, upsetting the carefully arranged pillows. She realized that, except for the nightly bad dreams, she'd had a peaceful week doing what she loved best.

THE PHONE on the night stand rang, and Laura reached across the pillows to retrieve it. The caller was

Chris Pfeifer, asking if she'd given any more thought to the rock-throwing incident.

"I've been concentrating on *not* thinking about it."

"Good survival strategy," he said. "But we need to put a stop to whoever's stalking you."

"Stalking? I hadn't thought of it that way," she said. "I guess the word fits, though."

"Absolutely."

"How are you sleeping?" he asked.

"Not."

"That's normal."

"I remembered something that I forgot to tell you earlier." She mentioned the note she'd found when she returned to the house after the snowstorm.

"Son of a bitch, Laura!"

"All this other stuff hadn't happened at the time."

"Of course. That makes sense," he said. "Excuse the language."

"I've used a few cuss words myself these past weeks. I'm hoping the cat doesn't pick them up," she said in a feeble attempt at humor.

'What was the date that you found the first note?"

Everyone in town could remember the dates of the recent snowstorm. She thought back and was able to pinpoint the date.

"Then, the bank robbery suspect was still with us when the note appeared," Pfeifer reminded her. "I'm not trying to insult you, but are you sure there was a first note and it wasn't part of one of the nightmares."

"I think I'm sure," she said. "What's this 'suspect' stuff?" she asked. "We both know he's guilty."

"He's accused," Pfeifer said patiently. "He hasn't gone to trial."

"And, how did you know I'm having nightmares?"

She hadn't told anyone that sometimes late at night she woke up with a start and thought someone was in the house. Or that sometimes during her waking hours she wondered if she'd seen the man in the get-away car in a dream or in real life.

"You'd be unusual if all this wasn't affecting your sleep. It's normal."

"Thanks. I need to hear that."

"Frankly, Roberts has been leery about your report of a possible get-away car. But, if there is a second man still at large, he could have had access to your house during that storm," he said. "And he'd have something to gain by keeping you quiet."

114

"And, it would mean that I didn't dream the black car," she said.

"We may be looking at two suspects in the bank robbery after all."

"And now they're both out there. Great," she said.

"I don't think John Smith would chance doing something even as small as tossing a rock through a window. His lawyer would have been forceful when he talked with him. Thanks to the Oregon voters, Measure Eleven sets minimum sentences for certain felonies. Smith's not going to chance racking up any additional charges on top of those we've got on him."

"It's a bathroom, not a theme park. Fresh walls and new towels will do it."

15

Aunt Esther and Laura swapped sections of *The Oregonian* they were reading during morning break. Esther reached for the comics while Laura bypassed most of the sports stories.

"Laura, I've been thinking about your Peeping Tom," Esther said.

"I try *not* to think about him."

"I don't think it's random," Esther said. "I mean, who runs around neighborhoods peeking into windows until he sees an attractive woman."

"And a surly cat," Laura added.

"I think it's got to be someone you've met. Have you thought about the people at the bank that day?"

"You and the cops. They quizzed me about the bank employees, and even expected me to have noticed their shoe sizes."

"Did you come up with any suspects?"

"My first thought," Laura said, "was the big guy who took down the robber. The cops got all excited about that potential lead. But, they investigated and found that the guy took a job on a fishing trawler out of Astoria the week after the bank robbery."

"Cross him off the list."

"Gone."

"Unless he got fired," Esther pondered aloud. "How 'bout bank employees?"

"They were mostly women," Laura said.

"That'd be an interesting twist."

"The employees' personal lifestyles aren't any of my business. But Roberts reported that he ran a check on the only man teller. He reported that the teller and his male partner don't appear to be likely suspects in this particular incident. And, as for the guard, he was a sawed-off guy, maybe 5' 5". He couldn't possibly wear a size 13 or 14 shoe."

"I wouldn't give this a rest if I were you," Esther said. "From now on, whenever you see a man you know, drop something on the ground so you can quickly stoop down and see how big his feet are."

"I'll take that into consideration," Laura said.

"No you won't," said a disappointed Esther. "I can tell by the tone of your voice."

IT WAS THE FOURTH time Laura had answered the phone in the past half hour that afternoon at The Harrington. She liked to think of the trips across the room to answer the landline as an exercise routine: bend, rise, walk, talk, bend, rise, walk . . .

She'd fended off the eager salesman from Sears who called to persuade her to update the warranty on a refrigerator she no longer owned. She politely turned down the telemarketer who offered her a weekend for two to look at vacation timeshares in eastern Oregon. With some regret she told college sophomore Heather that she couldn't contribute to the University of Oregon fundraiser this year. Though, she thought the U of O duck mascot was cute. . .

Laura let the next incoming call go to the answering machine.

"Can I drop by?" asked a deep masculine voice being recorded as he spoke.

She leaped from the couch and picked up the phone.

"Russ?" she asked.

"Or someone using my voice," he said.

"Good morning."

"I've got photos of the tiny house with me, Laura, and I need help picking out the exterior colors."

"Give me five minutes," she said. She hung up the phone and went upstairs to comb her hair and change from the ratty grey sweatshirt to a presentable black top with a muted tan and white striped long-sleeved shirt over it. The slim cut jeans she was wearing when the phone rang were fine. She shoved the furry slippers under the bed.

She was still barefoot when she heard the familiar knock on the front door, and walked down the stairs slowly to welcome Russ.

"What are you doing out and about today?"

"I keep making mental lists of what's left to do at the tiny house and how few days I have left to work on it before we're back to work for real," he said. "I needed some air."

He sat down at the dining room table and opened the laptop computer he carried with him. Photos of the quaint house popped up on the screen.

"My sunroom!" she squealed. "I mean '*a* sunroom," she corrected herself.

"*Your* sunroom is part of the dilemma," he said. "I'm trying to choose exterior colors. Should the framing around those sunroom windows be the same color as the siding or a different color?"

"Monsieur," she said. "That second color is known as an accent color," she said in her best imitation of a French accent. "And I'd have to see the main paint color to know."

"I want the structure to blend into the natural setting, yet make its own bold statement at the same time."

"What color is the roof?" she asked.

"Yet another problem," he said. "I was thinking of using charcoal textured shingles. Then, while I was at Copeland's Lumber Yard, I saw rust-colored tin roofing. I like the looks of it."

"I think you're talking about 'burnt sienna,' and it would be wonderful."

"If I use that colored roofing, can I still use evergreen stain on the wood siding?"

"Absolutely," she said. "I've taught you well."

"Now, here's the dilemma," he said.

"I thought the roof color was the big question."

"The big question today . . ." he said. (As opposed to the big question the last time we were at the lake, he thought.) ". . . is do I go bold and use a bright color on the trim and front entry door or do I play it safe and paint those dark brown?"

"A dark Hersey chocolate would be safe to the max," she said. "Of course, there's nothing wrong with being safe," she advised, remembering his constant safety reminders to her at the job sites.

"Why do I sense a 'however' coming?"

"The inside's still going to stay light natural wood. Right?" she confirmed.

Russ nodded.

"Then why not be fanciful on the outside?"

No response.

"Fanciful doesn't translate as feminine," she added.

"Oh. Then tell me more."

"If I were going to live there. . ." she started.

"Soon, I hope," he said. He waited silently for her to complete the sentence her way.

"I'd do the trim in an ocher yellow. Then, I'd pop the front door with a coat of OSU orange."

"You're serious?"

"You asked."

She walked across the room and returned with her deck of color chips.

"The trick," she said, "is to look at these colors in the proportions that they would be on the house. Expose the whole color chip that you're thinking of using for the exterior walls. Now put about a fourth of the 'roof chip' next to it."

"They look good together."

"Right," she said. "It's what I do for a living."

He added a small portion of the ocher color chip to the mix. "Still OK," he said.

"OSU orange may be a little much, after all," she said, nixing her own earlier suggestion. "This is why God made color chips."

"How about wine instead for the door?"

"Merlot or Chablis?" she asked.

"Merlot. Definitely merlot."

"You're getting really good at this," she told him. "The colors are spunky, not funky." She moved the color samples around on the table top again. "These colors will be really sweet in the fall when the leaves turn color. They're whimsical without being ridiculous."

"Just following what you've taught me. Near neutrals for walls and roof, one color for the trim, and a third color for the front door," he recited. "Only I ignored your roof rule this time."

A man who listens . . .

It was a new concept for Laura. She couldn't wait to tell Louise.

"If you're going small, go big with color schemes and decor."

16

Laura and Russ both regretted seeing their hiatus from work come to an end. They drove out to the site where the next Graham Construction Co. house was scheduled to be built. The lot was on a cul-de-sac with vacant land on both sides of it and to the rear where a mature grove of oak trees whispered in the wind. She was picturing a tire swing hanging from one of the lower branches of the nearest tree. She wondered if current safety rules nixed rope and tire swings for kids.

A tree house would be nice, too, she thought.

"What?" Russ asked when he saw the brooding look on her face

"Are kids still allowed to have rope swings," she asked.

"Probably not," he said. "But, I've been known to absent-mindedly leave an old tire in the newly finished garage. Let the parents weigh the liability against the joy of letting a kid have a normal childhood."

They circled the site once more before she admitted that she still didn't understand which way the windows would face on the ample but awkwardly-shaped lot. After this morning's tour she would spend the next few days drawing diagrams showing how the natural light would enter each room of the floor plan. Studying those would influence her interior design decisions.

Russ patiently took her by the hand and walked her around the property again. Next, he produced the plans, rolled them out between his outstretched hands, and outlined the floor plan for the future house.

Laura suspected that the architect had a lapse in judgment when he placed two fireplaces at the same end of the house.

"Wouldn't it save money and be more dramatic to have a see-through fireplace on the partial wall between the living and dining rooms?" she asked.

"Smart lady," Russ said. "Tell me more."

She favored cork or bamboo flooring, also, but some of their clients hadn't yet made the move to that eco-friendly choice. Surprising for Oregonians, she thought.

Laura felt more grounded as they talked about the return to a daily work routine together. Very little about her free days in January and February had turned out to be the relaxing time she had anticipated.

"DID EITHER of you sublet the workshop?" Esther asked as she came in the door to work the next morning.

The question caught Russ and Laura by surprise and neither answered.

"Everyone awake this morning?" Esther asked. "Don't make me get out the harmonica."

"Awake. Absolutely awake," Russ said quickly.

"Why would we rent out the workshop?" Laura asked.

"There seems to be a young couple coming and going from there after dark."

"You're kidding me," Russ said.

"Did you recognize them?" Laura asked.

"No, and I don't plan to introduce myself either," Esther said. "Two teenage skunks, brazen as could be, strolled across the yard last night and disappeared under the wooden steps. I smelled 'em coming."

"It's the right time of year for skunks," Russ said.

"It's never a right time of year for skunks," Esther responded. "And definitely not when I live above the workshop."

"What do people do to discourage skunks?" Laura asked.

"I already did it," Esther said. "I called Skunks Are Us. They're listed in the yellow pages and they promise results."

"Are they a no-kill operation?"

"This is a don't-ask-don't-tell situation," Esther responded. "Stella, the skunk lady, will be out here this afternoon to set some live traps. After these guys leave with her, it's her call what she does with them."

"Are you comfortable with that?" Laura asked.

"The choice is black and white to me."

"She set you up for that one," Russ said.

"Black and white remains an elegant and sophisticated choice in decor."

17

Esther swung her older Honda Element into the parking area between her residence and Graham Construction. She was surprised to see another car parked off to the side. She knew it hadn't been there when she'd headed toward the Fred Meyer shopping center at 9 p.m. to purchase cookie dough ice cream and a can of butter toffee peanuts.

Russ and Laura were both out at separate activities for the evening so she had planned to munch her favorite snacks in peace while a Red Box movie played on her TV.

That was the plan.

"Did I leave the lights on?" Esther wondered aloud as she reached across the front car seat to pick up the bag of snacks. She climbed out of the car and glanced upstairs toward her front entry door.

Esther stopped mid-step.

There were lights coming from every room in her apartment above the workshop. She hunted in her purse for her cell phone, but remembered she had left it on the nightstand in her bedroom. Inside the apartment.

She dug in her purse and found the key to the workshop on a separate key ring. Skunks be damned, she thought. She unlocked the door and slipped into the workshop quietly. She set the grocery bag on the workbench and used the laser light on her regular keychain to see which hand tools were spread out on the workbench. She selected her weapon of choice and quietly left the workshop, leaving the door ajar so the noise of the latch closing wouldn't alert whoever was in her house that they were about to have company.

She moved quietly up the exterior stairs and stood to the side of the window, hoping her tennis shoes wouldn't be heard on each step. When she reached the top stair and turned slightly to peer in the front window, she could see someone leaning against the breakfast counter. He had his back to her. She could hear muffled voices so she assumed there was more than one person present.

"Whoever they are, they weren't invited," she said to herself.

She stepped through the door and saw the backs of two men, neither of whom she recognized from the rear.

"Put your hands above your heads and don't move," she commanded.

The men seemed startled, but did as instructed. She noted that they were well-dressed. If she'd seen them on the street she'd have guessed chiropractor and actuary, she thought randomly.

"Keep your hands up or I'll shoot," she threatened. "You on the left," she said to the shorter one. "Slowly turn around."

He did as instructed and she addressed the second intruder. "Now you."

The first man took a step forward and Esther pointed the weapon at him.

"It's an effen staple gun," he said.

"This is not any ol' staple gun," she said. "It's a Stanley TR250 SharpShooter."

He took a second step and Esther fired, sending the heavy duty staple through the top of his right shoe and into his foot.

"She shot me! Damn that hurts! The Bitch shot me!"

"Shut up, Bernie," his companion said, freezing in place.

"There's blood in my shoe. She can't do that! Are you just going to stand there?"

"What do you expect me to do?"

131

"*I* expect both of you keep your hands up and your mouths shut. Otherwise the next shot will be three feet higher and six inches to the right," Esther threatened. "*Capiche?*"

She'd never spoken Italian in her life, but she liked the sound of the word. Maybe she'd use it more often, she thought. She moved sideways toward the lamp table and reached for the telephone on it. She put the receiver to her ear while holding the gun with her right hand. The phone was dead.

"You idiots," she said. "You two cut the wires to the landline? Good grief. Everyone has a cell phone now days. Isn't that right?" she asked the man called Bernie.

He nodded automatically.

"Great! Take *yours* out of your pocket slowly and carefully and toss it on that chair."

He followed her orders. Both intruders watched helplessly as she picked up the cell phone and dialed 911.

"I'd like to report two burglars in my house," she said. "I'm holding them at gunpoint."

She waved the staple gun at the two men to signal that she meant business.

The dispatcher heard a loud noise.

"What was that? Are you there, ma'am?"

Esther had absentmindedly squeezed the trigger on the gun and a staple whizzed past the taller man's head and shattered the pottery cookie jar resting on the window ledge several feet behind him.

"Misfire," Esther explained. "My bad."

"Everyone's OK, then?" the dispatcher asked.

"Fine for now."

"The officers are on the way. They should be arriving any minute, ma'am. We had a car in your area."

"I hear it now. Sounds like it's pulling into the parking lot below," Esther responded.

"I want you to be ready to peacefully relinquish your weapon to the officers as soon as you see that they have the situation under control," the dispatcher told her. "That's very important."

"Will do," Esther said. "But, if these two idiots move so much as a muscle before then, I'm going to fill them full of lead—two tiny holes at a time."

"Police!" an officer yelled. "Making entry!"

Two uniformed officers stepped into Esther's small quarters. Each had his gun drawn.

"Are you hurt, ma'am?" an officer asked. He reached for the staple gun Esther held without taking his eyes off the two men. "Keep your hands up, gentlemen. I'm Officer Ryan. My partner Officer Daniels is going to cuff you for our safety and yours until we know what's going on here."

"Is it OK if I sit down now?" Esther asked.

"Were you the one who called in?"

Esther nodded. "I live here," she said. "I'm the one who called you, but I commandeered one of their phones to use," she said and passed the cell phone to the officer.

"Take a seat and try to relax."

He turned to the two men. "We're going to frisk you and check your pockets, gentlemen. We'll put the contents, including your ID, on the counter."

Esther watched as they placed small change, one handkerchief, a couple of stubs from the movie theater, two pocket knives, an over-sized paper clip, and a small tin of aspirin on the stack.

"Got a toothache," the man called Bernie said to no one in particular.

The officers then added two wallets to the collection on the counter.

Esther looked across at the stack of items. "No pocket lint," she said. "Those pants must have to be dry-cleaned." That confirmed her earlier suspicion that these were not practiced thugs and didn't have a clue about the appropriate work attire for tonight's break-in.

The officers ignored the comment.

"Your name, sir?" one of them asked the shorter man.

"Bernard Alfred Rosen."

"And, you sir?" the cop asked the second man. He picked up the two drivers licenses from the counter top to verify their answers.

"Clyde. Clyde Lewis Fredrickson."

"Bernie and Clyde?" Esther asked. "For real?"

The first officer double checked the drivers' licenses. "For real," he repeated.

"Occupation?" he asked suspect Bernard Rosen.

"Attorney at Law."

"More like disbarred now," his friend Clyde said.

"Shut up!" Bernie said under his breath.

"And, *your* occupation, sir?" the officer asked.

Clyde Frederickson hesitated. He opened his mouth to respond once, but then apparently changed his mind. There was an extended pause. "Entrepreneur," he said eventually. "I owned a chain of men's clothing stores."

"Yeah. He's not your everyday storekeeper. Clyde was president of the local businessmen's association," Bernie said.

"Zip it, you ass," Clyde said.

"Mrs. Graham, have you ever seen either of these gentlemen before tonight when you returned to your residence?"

"Never."

"So, it follows that they didn't have your permission to be inside your dwelling?" he asked.

"Absolutely not," Esther responded. "Though I was warned, if I wiped out the skunks, the rats would follow."

"Neither this one nor the one who's hopping around on one foot?" the officer asked.

"No sir," she said. "Hoppy might need a suture or a butterfly bandage on that foot, though."

"We'll have 'medical' take a look at it when we take them in," he said.

"And, do you see anything missing from your residence on first inspection?"

Esther wandered into the small bedroom and glanced in the bathroom.

"No, sir," she said.

"You can contact us later if you discover something missing."

"I want to press charges," she said.

"Well, ma'am, you don't have to do that. You reported the incident and Officer Ryan and I have completed a preliminary investigation of that report. The charges will be filed by the Bureau," he told her. "Those charges won't be formally in place until we've completed our investigation, but it's not looking good for these two tonight."

Both officers left their business cards on the small entryway table and escorted the two hand-cuffed men carefully down the staircase to the patrol car.

Esther heard the car doors slam and the police car pull out of the lot. She remembered then that there was ice cream secreted in a plain brown paper bag in the workshop below. She waited two minutes to make sure the police cruiser wasn't returning, then rescued the snacks.

WHEN LAURA called the next day to find out more about the incident at Esther's house, the officers told her that the two suspects would be refused bail while the detectives assigned to the case determined whether there was any truth to the intruders' story that there had been a simple misunderstanding about the address.

"They've admitted they made entry illegally, but they're claiming they were to meet a 'colleague' and got the wrong address.'

"Is that plausible?" she asked.

"With the amount of cash each of them had on his person, we suspect their so-called colleague was most likely their cocaine source."

"You're kidding me," she said.

"One of the officers saw small plastic sleeves with white powder in the suspects' wallets when he searched them last night. He slipped those into an evidence bag out of sight of Mrs. Graham who was still eyeing her staple gun."

"Smart man," Laura said. "Glad I called. I think having this information will help Esther," Laura told him. "She was awake most of the night wondering why they'd chosen her small home to rob."

She didn't tell him that Esther had said several times during breakfast that, had she been the police, she would have "hung the bastards first and asked questions later."

"Granite counters don't necessarily rock."

18

When Laura and Esther approached, Ernie and Russ grew quiet. The men were standing outside the side door to Graham Construction.

"You two look like you each swallowed a different part of the canary," Esther said.

"We were trying to decide what we want on our sandwiches if Ernie makes a run to Subway. Are you two hungry?"

"Not for a sandwich," Esther said. "But, I'd throw in a few dollars for their chocolate chip cookie platter."

"Essie, why don't you come with me to help carry things?" Ernie suggested. The red jeep roared out of the driveway with Esther's scarf blowing in the wind and Russ and Laura left behind.

"Why'd you both look so guilty if all you were talking about was dill pickles and mustard or mayo?" Laura asked.

"You caught us," he said. "They haven't announced it yet, but Ernie and Esther are getting married. Ernie wasn't supposed to tell me, but he slipped."

"You're kidding me."

"Remember to act surprised when they tell you this afternoon," he said

"I'm not sure I'm that good an actress."

"You better be or Ernie and I are in big trouble here."

LAURA WHOOPED when Ernie and Esther announced their engagement half an hour later at an "engagement party" for four with the future bridegroom serving submarine sandwiches, small bags of potato chips and cookies.

"Are you eloping or having a formal wedding?" Russ asked.

"We'll probably scoot down to the courthouse on our morning break one day," Esther said.

"Not on our watch," Laura said. "Why don't you let us gather a few friends together and Russ and I can host a small garden wedding at The Harrington?"

Russ nodded in agreement.

140

"We wouldn't want you to go to all that trouble," Ernie said.

"Oh, I don't know," Esther put in. "It might be kind of fun. It'd be much classier than posing for a photo with the bums in Pioneer Square near the courthouse." She turned toward Laura. "You just happen to have a small English garden?"

"That I do!" Laura said. "I promise we'll keep the occasion simple but memorable. I'll need a month or so to get the yard in shape."

"We're not in any hurry, are we?" Ernie asked Esther.

"No, but I don't want Laura to exhaust herself fussing over this."

THE NO-FUSS WEDDING was in danger of getting out of hand. Laura was keeping her part of the deal. She'd spent a few hours planting annuals in the flower beds around the back patio. Those would be in bloom along with the spring bulbs by the day of the ceremony. She asked Russ to use a power washer on the back walkway and fence. She hired a local handyman to freshen the white paint on the gazebo. Then, she sat back and listened to Esther and Ernie fuss over the bride's choice of bouquet and the menu for a light dinner for the few guests they had agreed to invite.

"We need your help on this," Ernie said. "What flowers would you choose?"

"Me?" Laura asked. "I'd carry a white nosegay."

"Perfect," the future bride said.

"And, if it was my wedding," Laura said, "I'd ask that bridegroom of yours to make his famous lasagna, green salad and home-baked bread for a casual meal after you've exchanged vows."

As best man and maid of honor, Russ and Laura volunteered to be the legal witnesses. That solved one problem, but now the bridal couple was insisting on splitting up to shop for wedding attire.

Ernie asked Russ to help him find a fashionable suit so he didn't have to wear the one he'd purchased for a funeral in 1999.

Esther roped Laura into driving with her to a nearby bridal shop to select a dress that didn't "look like an old lady who rose from the dead to tie the knot." Esther purchased a blush colored suit with a cream lace high-necked camisole to go under the jacket. She declared it "perfect" and noted that it made her look ten pounds slimmer and five years younger. Or was it five pounds thinner and ten years younger, she debated.

Laura had admired a dress when they first entered the store. The soft yellow dress complimented her auburn hair and coloring perfectly. While she agreed with bride-to-be Esther that the dress was gorgeous, she thought it was a little fussy for a maid of honor.

"Nonsense," Esther said. "Trust me. You'll always wish you'd bought that dress if you walk out of here without it."

Laura was too tired to argue and purchased the dress without bothering to try it on in the store.

Ernie asked Laura on the sly if she could help him pick out a wedding ring Esther would like.

Esther offered to bake a cake, but couldn't decide whether tiny statues of two grey-haired senior citizens in wedding attire mired in the frosting would be appropriate. And, was the frosting going to be butter cream, fondant, whipped glaze or marzipan? She was holding off on that decision until closer to day of the impending nuptials. Yet, she asked daily what kind of icing Laura would prefer.

THE OFFICERS who had been at Esther's the night "Bernie and Clyde" broke in returned to Esther's apartment to update her on the two men who were arrested.

"This was a case that started with mistaken identity," Officer Daniels said.

"You're telling me I have a doppelganger in town?" Esther asked.

"No. Not you, the house. There's another home in the area with an apartment above a garage in the rear. It looks very similar to this property."

"At least it did in the dark," Officer Ryan added. "They entered the wrong apartment."

"They're both still guilty of breaking and entering, but they're not your everyday thugs," Daniels said. "At one time these jokers were both well respected business men in the community."

"That explains the suits," Esther said.

"The suspects took a dive when they got into drugs. They each wound up divorced, living in a downtown hotel, splitting the rent. Clyde's a talker. He admitted they'd pooled their last resources that night for a drug buy."

"That doesn't speak well for our neighborhood," Esther said.

"Now days it could be any neighborhood," Ryan said. "They gave up the address and name of their dealer in exchange for plea deals that include limited jail time and mandated drug rehab."

Esther was quiet after the officers left. She was thinking about the interesting possibilities if she had actually had a double.

"Hello. I'm Essie and this is my doppelganger Bessie Harplehanger."

"There is no such thing as a low-key wedding. Wedding planners earn their fee one silky bow and one sulky bride at a time."

19

Laura moved the groceries from the truck to the side porch two bags at a time. She hadn't planned to buy out the place, but everything in the grocery department looked appetizing tonight.

That's why they tell you not to shop when you're hungry, she thought. Whoever "they" are.

She next swung the shopping bags through the door and onto the kitchen counter. She dropped the last bring-it-yourself bright green cloth shopping bag there and wondered belatedly if that was the one that contained the egg carton.

Plastic bags were taboo in environmentally friendly Portland. There was a day, Laura remembered, when a woman could frost her hair at home with a crochet hook and a plastic bag. Probably not any more. Especially now with a Neighborhood Watch Group on the street. . .

She set the last bag on the kitchen counter, dropped her raincoat to the floor, and turned toward the table.

A man was sitting there.

He had a gun, and it was pointed at her.

A knife sat on the table near his left hand.

"I beg your pardon," she said.

"Take a seat at the table," he said. "Nothing funny. Just sit."

"Is that one of my new steak knives?" she asked. "Did you get that from the butcher block knife holder on the counter?"

"Sit!"

She sat.

"Are you sure you have the right house?" she asked. "Many of them along this row look alike."

She noticed that he had helped himself to a box of graham crackers and a jar of peanut butter from her pantry and had been eating a snack while he waited for her. A can of Coke sat next to the crackers. No napkin, she noticed.

He was wearing a heavy jacket and a ski mask. He either mumbled when he talked or the mask was getting in his way.

When the man didn't answer, she said, "Well, make yourself at home."

"I did. Nobody needs to get hurt if you do as you're told."

"That's a line right out of a movie," she said.

"Shut up, bitch."

"How do you spell that?" she asked, her thoughts shifting to the note wrapped around the rock that had shattered the front window.

"Spell what?"

She sensed he was growing agitated. "Never mind," she said. "Not all that important. Why don't you tell me why you're here."

"This isn't no social call."

"I gathered that already," she said. She glanced over her shoulder at the door.

"You'd never make it," he said and pointed the gun at her again. "You saw me at the bank that day. Sure, you jumped back on the curb, but you already seen me."

She was tempted to correct his grammar, but something told her this was not the time.

"No. No. I didn't see anything but the car and I didn't see it clearly."

"You're lying."

"Well, maybe a little," she said. "Since I already saw you," she lied, "why don't you ditch that itchy ski mask."

149

He yanked it off and jammed it in a jacket pocket.

She'd never seen such a non-descript man in her life. Medium height, average weight, no distinguishing features. Medium brown hair and nondescript brown eyes. Caucasian. No scars. No tattoos. His chin receded a little more than some, but not enough to distinguish him from a thousand other mug shots she'd be asked to view if she lived through this impromptu visit in her kitchen.

"Does your mother know what you do for a living?" she asked.

"Leave my Mom out of this. I only agreed to drive the car for a split of the cash to pay the old lady's rent."

"You sound like a wonderful son," Laura tried.

"If I was a wonderful son, she wouldn't be living in that dump."

"Well, things happen . . ." Laura started.

"Here's what's gonna happen here. You keep your mouth shut about the getaway car and I'll figure out some other way to get the old lady into a group home."

Her cell phone rang, startling them both.

"Don't answer that," he said.

"It's probably my boyfriend," she told him.

"Of course it is," he said. "And next you're gonna tell me that he's 6'7" and 350 pounds and on his way here to throw me to the ground and sit on me. Don't pick up."

"He's the suspicious type. If I don't answer, he'll be at the door in no time."

He thought a minute. "OK. Pick up, but get rid of him. This knife can slit your throat in one quick stroke."

Laura noted that he'd chosen a knife with a serrated edge. A perfect selection for slicing an herbed pork tenderloin. Or her throat.

She looked at the Caller ID screen that said "UNIDENTIFIED CALLER." The calls she'd taken in the past from the police bureau had shown the same words. She picked up the phone and leaned against the kitchen wall, facing the armed man who was now toying with the wood-handled steak knife.

"Hello," she said quietly.

"Pfeifer here."

"Hi, Honey," she said. "I was hoping you'd call. Would you mind stopping at the grocery store on your way home?"

"Laura?"

"It's not a long list. Do you have a lead pencil?"

"Laura, what's wrong?"

"I wouldn't ask, but I forgot these things."

"Shoot," he said, still confused.

"Oh, could you?" she answered. "Do you have a lead pencil? O.K. Here goes: Smith Brothers cough drops, and Wesson oil. . ."

"Do the brands matter?" he asked.

"Today? Absolutely."

"That's it?"

"I just remembered. We also need pepper and hairspray. That ought to do it."

"Are you OK out there?" he asked.

"I miss you too, Babycakes." She hung up the phone.

"BABYCAKES?" Pfeifer repeated. He sat quietly at his desk, trying to figure out why Laura Howard would be talking nonsense. Calls coming into the Police Bureau were automatically recorded. He asked the "tech" on duty to listen to this one with him.

"Is she a native speaker?" the technician asked when the taped conversation ended.

"As far as I know," Pfeifer said.

"Listen to it again, Babycakes."

"That's the last time you call me that. What are you hearing that I missed?"

"The emphasized words," the technician said. "One more time. I'll write them down while you listen." He started the recorded message again.

"Lead. Smith. And. Wesson," he said as he wrote. "Pepper. Spray," the technician repeated as he jotted down the last two words. "Plus, she begs you to shoot."

"Damn!" Pfeifer yelled as he bolted from the chair to call dispatch.

LAURA LOOKED down at her hands. They were shaking. No surprise there, she thought.

"You did very well on that call," her uninvited guest told her. "You got anything stronger than Coke here?" he asked.

"No." she said. "You do know it won't take Joe more than ten minutes to get here with those groceries. You've had your snack. You've delivered your message. It's time for you to go. And I mean right now!"

He stared in disbelief at the assertive order.

"Oooh, I'm so scared." He cocked the gun and stared at her menacingly. "Shut up or you'll be as dead as those flowers I ran over."

She ignored his threat, but knew now who had destroyed the parkway garden at The Harrington.

Something snapped in Laura. It was *her* house, *her* kitchen. She'd had all she could take.

"You've eaten," she repeated. "You've scared me with the gun. Now get out of here before someone gets hurt."

"Listen here. . ."

"No, you listen. I've had it up to here with bank robberies, replacing windows, burying murdered plants, and now this. I got your message. I'm not stupid."

Laura was as surprised as he was when she took her stand. This was either the spunky Laura who used to live at The Harrington or Idiot Girl who had almost gotten herself shot at the bank a few weeks ago.

"I have no intention of going to the police," she said. "The only one who is going anywhere is you. Now!"

He glanced through the archway between the kitchen the dining room and out the front window.

"Damn! You're right! I'm outta here," he said. "You keep it zipped!"

Laura wasn't sure she'd been that convincing, but she was glad he was leaving, no matter what the reason.

Three police cars had pulled up in front of the house without colored lights flashing or sirens sounding at the exact minute that the intruder had looked outside. He tucked the gun in his waistband, grabbed the can of Coke and the knife and ran toward the back door.

"Leave the knife," she yelled. "It's part of a matched set."

He tossed it toward the sink before he left, letting the door slam behind him. She hadn't seen the police cars out front and was silently congratulating herself at how well her assertiveness had worked.

She heard his car roar to life and shoot up to the next side street. The cops were at her front door a minute later. There was a loud knock at the door.

"Police!"

She ushered the Portland officers inside. She wasn't pretending to be brave this time. She didn't care that she was crying. And she didn't care if the tears were because she was scared or because she was mad. She interrupted the lead officer's first question to describe the situation she'd endured in the kitchen the past twenty minutes. He signaled to two officers who exited quickly in pursuit of the intruder who was probably a dozen city blocks away by now.

Laura described the incident in detail, stopping only to quell a sniff or two. A young officer took notes as she talked. She reminded them of the last two incidents, the rock thrown through her front window and the slaughter of the tree and flowers.

"You can check with Detective Chris Pfeifer for the history of all this," she said. "I'm not some loony who imagines an armed man in her kitchen eating crackers and peanut butter. He was here when I came in the back door. He had a knife and he had a gun he was waving around like a lunatic."

"Was it loaded?"

Laura stared at the young officer.

"How long have you been with the Portland police department?" she asked, her voice rising. "How would I know if it was loaded? If someone points a gun at you and tells you to keep quiet, would you ask if he took time to load the gun?"

"Sorry, ma'am."

"If Pfeifer hadn't been on the ball, I'd be dead right now."

"I understand, ma'am."

"You know, I'm through for tonight. He's gone," she said. "*You* think I'm old enough to be addressed as 'ma'am' and your two colleagues are trying to capture someone who squealed off in his car before they could get their own keys out of the ignition"

"I understand," he repeated.

"No, I don't think you do. I used to be cooperative and understanding and appreciate the tough job you

156

have to do. But, tonight I'm through," she said. "If you need any other information, ask Detectives Pfeifer or Roberts to call me in the morning. I'm locking all the doors, eating the carrot cake I brought home, setting the alarm, and going to bed."

The young cop was speechless.

"Don't let the cat out."

"HELLO, MS. HOWARD," the voice on the phone said. "This is Leonard Roberts. I hear you had a harrowing experience last night."

"That's one way to describe it."

"Did you get any indication that the intruder could have been linked to the two recent acts of vandalism at your home?" he asked.

"Absolutely. He pretty much told me so. This guy isn't among the overly bright. That was what made it so frightening. That and the gun he had pointed at me."

"That must have been terrifying," Roberts said. "It sounds like he was out of control."

"As Esther says 'there's dumb, and then there's damn dumb.' This guy was the second."

"What makes you think that?"

"There's no way I could have identified him from the quick glimpse I got of him when he was in his car roaring

157

past me near the bank. After suggesting he take off the ski mask and, then, watching him eat every snack in my kitchen, I now know *exactly* what he looks like."

"Smart lady," he said. "So you can describe him?"

"Yes, but it won't be too helpful."

"Why's that?"

"He's average in every way but brains," she said. "Not handsome, not ugly."

"Agreed. That's a little vague so far," Roberts said.

"What can I say? He's nondescript. He's not going to win any beauty contests," she said.

"Go on."

"Mr. Congeniality is out of the picture, too."

"Not good for us. But, it's still terrifying for you until we nab the guy," Roberts said. "Is there anything we can do to help you until this thug is picked up?"

"Nothing I can think of," she started. "Oh, you could relay my apologies to a young officer I selected to unload my frustrations on last night."

"I'm sure the officer never noticed. We would expect someone held at gunpoint to be upset," he said. "You're sure there's nothing we can do to help until we have this guy locked up."

"I just want my life back," she said.

"We'll do our best. He left partial prints on the knife. The officers on the scene found it and bagged it," Roberts said. "We'll get that knife back to you as soon as we're through processing it. I can't believe he left it behind."

"I told him to."

"You what?" Roberts asked.

"I tend to babble in emergency situations."

"Well this time you may have babbled yourself right into a conviction for this jerk. Nice work."

"Thanks," she said quietly. "The knife was part of a set." She realized that information probably wasn't pertinent to Roberts. Oh, well.

"Maybe you could stay with one of your co-workers for a couple of nights while we hunt for the guy."

"That's probably good thinking."

"One other thing," he said.

Laura thought he sounded like old-time TV Detective Colombo.

"When I drove by your place after the front tree and flowers were destroyed, I noticed evidence to support something you told me a while back."

"What was that?"

"The flowers. Primroses, did you call them?" he asked. "They looked like they must have been beautiful.

159

A subtler purple and paler yellow than the patches on a Police Bureau uniform."

Laura thought she heard an apology somewhere in between those words.

They ended the call and she phoned Esther to ask for a reservation on the couch at her apartment for one distraught decorator and one feisty orange cat. She'd describe the reason for her stay when she got there, she told Esther. And, no, she didn't expect a mini fridge in the room.

"A chair-and-a-half seats a wit and a half."

20

Laura appreciated Esther's hospitality. Even without the harmonica music, though, the quarters were too small for two adults and a cat for much longer.

"Leaving already?" Esther asked as Laura made up the sleeper couch in the small living room.

"Russ had every lock at The Harrington re-keyed," Laura said. "Remind me to give you a key," she added. "And, the alarm company has been out to the house twice since the break-in. They're still not sure how the guy bypassed the alarm and got into my kitchen, but they guarantee me it can't happen again."

"Are they sure?" Esther asked. "Would any of them let *his* wife sleep there to test their repair work?"

"Sometimes you scare me, Esther. We're starting to think alike," Laura said. "I asked that, but their only

161

answer was to show me again how to arm and disarm the alarm."

"If you think it's safe to be there . . ."

"I have to admit that I don't have the same warm attachment to The Harrington now that I used to have," Laura said.

"Why would you after everything that's happened?"

"But, I do know that I have to force myself to live in the world and not cower in a corner, dreading what might happen next."

"That's logical, but feelings and logic aren't always in sync," Esther said. "Do you want to take the harmonica with you in case the alarm malfunctions?"

LAURA CHANGED her clothes, applied lip gloss, and pulled her hair back into a low pony tail. She'd dressed to blend into a crowd. That was her fashion goal for today.

Her more worthy goal was to start reclaiming her life. She couldn't stay locked up in the house wondering what the next calamity might be.

She walked out to the truck parked at the curb in front of the house, hopped in, and drove to the nearest movie theater.

"What better place to go to conquer a fear of the dark?" she had asked Louise when she first thought of the idea. This new attempt to conquer her fear of being alone reminded her of the early months after Todd Howard's death when she had to teach herself to comfortably dine out alone. Surely, going to a movie theater solo would be easier than that had been. Here, no one else could see if she faltered. And, she could order buttered popcorn instead of an over-priced soup and salad.

THE MOVIE WAS a disappointment to Laura.

Why do they lace every third sentence with the "F" word? The plot wasn't all that strong, but it didn't need vulgarity to carry it along, she thought. It had been a long time since she'd been to a show. Were Disney movies still safe? Did Cinderella now yell profanities at the mice and her fairy godmother?

She'd conquered eating out alone after Todd died. Maybe that would remain her only solo achievement for a while. She'd indulge herself with a cheeseburger at the McDonalds' window on the way home and wait for another time to conquer her new fears. Be wild, she thought. Ask the cook to add tomato and guacamole. . .

She walked out of the theater lobby directly behind two middle-aged couples. Both Russ and Chris Pfeifer had cautioned her often enough about avoiding dark parking lots alone at night so she walked directly behind the couples, as an uninvited fifth member.

The five of them moved across the lot together, then separated to walk toward their vehicles that had each been carefully parked beneath separate overhead lights. Did these couples know Pfeifer and Russ too? Or were they also safety fanatics, she wondered.

She checked behind the truck seat before she got in, entered the cab with her keys held between her knuckles as a weapon, and locked the doors. She put the key in the ignition and moved the truck slowly out of the parking lot and onto the main street.

Laura knew she could arrive home faster by taking a shortcut through side streets, but she was still practicing being a "together adult" tonight. She'd stick with the four-lane arterial boulevard.

The car behind her was following closer than was comfortable, she noticed.

Laura decided that the driver behind her was probably another woman whose male friends had her so spooked about driving alone after dark that she wasn't leaving room for some hood to cut her off.

Laura put her foot on the gas pedal when the next light turned green. She had convinced herself that she didn't care about the driver behind her. But, she sped up anyway.

The driver matched her speed.

Laura gunned it again at the next intersection.

The driver of the car shadowed her every move, changing lanes each time she did. Only this time, the car behind her got close enough to tap her back bumper.

"Hey," she yelled before remembering no one could hear her with the truck windows closed.

She considered reaching for her cell phone to call for help, but thought better of it when the car behind her hit the truck for a second time. *That* was no accident, she thought, as she absorbed the jolt. She needed to keep both hands on the steering wheel in case the idiot tried ramming her truck full force.

If she saw a police car, she'd hit the horn and put the cell phone to her ear in hopes he'd spot it and pull her over for "distracted driving."

She looked in the rearview mirror. The dark car was still there, now driving without headlights. Two more vehicles were about a half-block back in the outside lane. She put the truck's flashing lights on and began honking the horn to attract attention.

The only one who seemed to notice was the driver in pursuit who honked back at her. Surely there were noise ordinances in town at this time of night, she thought. Why isn't somebody reporting me?

The driver following at the rear of her truck dropped back for a moment, then sped up, blasted his car horn, swerved, and intentionally sideswiped the driver's side of the truck. The impact threw her truck out of control and it skidded up and over the curb and across the sidewalk, coming to a stop when the front right fender first struck and then went up and over a royal blue U.S. mailbox.

Both airbags inflated and Laura gasped for breath as white powdery dust sifted down on her. She coughed and gasped for air, inhaling more of the powder.

Other motorists reached the accident scene and pulled over immediately. A quick-thinking teenage boy rushed to the truck and pried the door open so she could get some air. Others used their cell phones to call for help.

THE POLICE WERE interviewing the observers while the paramedics evaluated Laura's injuries. She had remained seated in the cab while they took vital signs and asked pertinent questions about her degree of pain. Now they carefully eased her out of the truck.

It was dark and no one had been able to take down the license plate of the "attacking vehicle," but all of them agreed it was a small black compact car. One of those motorists had asked his passenger to call the police department the first time the car made contact with the back bumper of Laura's truck. That motorist had then dropped back a half block to avoid becoming involved in a three-car accident. He swore the first collision with her bumper had been intentional.

The police were two blocks back when the final collision occurred. The occupants of two police cruisers stopped to help Laura and to direct traffic around the truck which still rested with the right front side of the cab atop the mailbox. Two additional officers went "code three," turning on the sirens and lights on their cars, as they sped off in pursuit of the hit-and-run driver.

Laura was too shaken to object when an ambulance arrived to transport her to the hospital emergency room. The doctor and nurse there were thorough, but not chatty. Laura wondered if Esther had been a talkative emergency room nurse in her day. She suspected she knew the answer without asking.

"Down to Imaging for you," the ER doctor said. "It's the only way to tell if you have broken or bruised ribs. They present similarly."

Laura suspected "present similarly" was medical jargon for "hurt like heck." Her chest felt like a sumo wrestler was lounging on it.

When she was wheeled back through the emergency room to her assigned cubby, she heard two familiar voices. Russ and Pfeifer were sitting there visiting like two old ladies at a Sunday tea. She strained to overhear their conversation.

"The witness couldn't identify the car except to say it was small and dark," Pfeifer said.

"Another Scion?" Russ asked.

"That's not impossible. We never did locate the first one."

"How much damage is there to the truck? She loves that truck."

"The driver's side is scraped from the back fender clear up to the door. I can't figure out why the impact didn't flip her. He hit her pretty hard. There should be paint from the truck on the car that collided with her. That's a plus for us as we look for the driver," Pfeifer said.

"Some days I'm not sure I'm up to the responsibility of keeping Laura safe," Russ confided.

"Good luck with that one," Pfeifer said. "Until we contain this creep, you're going to need to be even more vigilant. Call us any time."

"Thanks," Russ said. "Did Laura say where she was coming from at this time of night?"

"She'd apparently gone to the movies."

"The movies?" Russ repeated. "Alone?"

"As I said, do your best, but call us any time." Pfeifer put his hat back on and gave Russ a friendly mock salute. "To serve and protect," he said, reciting the Portland Police Bureau motto. "Good luck."

"DID YOU SEE my truck?" Laura asked when Russ was admitted through the privacy curtain shielding her hospital bed. "How bad is it?" she asked. "And what were you and Pfeifer talking about?"

He ignored the questions and leaned down and kissed her on the forehead. "How is she?" he asked the doctor.

"She has a couple of cracked ribs," the doctor said. "She's going to be pretty sore."

"You didn't tell me that," Laura said.

"He asked first."

"And what were you and Pfeifer talking about out there?" Laura asked Russ again.

"I'll tell you later. He has a description of the car that plowed into you, but no license plate info."

"Tell me the truck's OK," she said.

"It will be by the time you see it again. I'll take it down to the body shop tomorrow." He didn't' want her to see it in its current condition. "Do you have collision insurance?"

"I've got every kind of insurance you can name. I don't always understand insurance policies, but if my agent Harvey recommends it, I've got it," she said. "How long will it take to fix the truck?"

"Doesn't matter," he said. "You won't be driving for a while. Trust me on this one. I've had broken ribs before and you're going to want to stay put."

Esther greeted them when they pulled up in front of The Harrington in Russ' truck. Russ helped Laura ease out of the passenger side. He could have predicted it would hurt when her feet hit the pavement, jarring her body.

"Damn!" she said. "You'll have to excuse me," she said immediately. "I saw an R-rated movie last tonight."

"And all you learned was 'damn?'" Esther asked. She turned to Russ. "Is she OK?"

"Pretty much," Russ said. "She escaped with a couple of injured ribs."

"Those are gonna hurt.'"

"Isn't there something you can put on ribs?" Laura asked Esther.

"Barbecue sauce?"

"Thanks for that professional advice. You sound like the doctor. He said I'll have to wait to 'cure.' I felt like a ham."

"Dust ruffles. Who needs them?"

21

The woman who had identified herself as Candace Galassi earlier in the month was back at the Graham Construction office. This time Laura answered the knock on the door.

"Oh, I thought Mr. Graham lived here," she said. "You're Laura Howard, aren't you?"

Russ walked into the room to see who had arrived. When Laura stepped aside, he moved toward the doorway.

"I thought I made it clear that no one at this site is interested in a television interview," he said.

"If I can't talk to one of you soon," the woman said, "there won't be a timely angle for the story anyway."

"I think we're all fine with that," Russ said.

Esther poked her head around the kitchen door to see who had arrived.

"I understand," Candace said to Russ. "If Laura Howard is too traumatized to talk with me, I'd be happy to meet with *you* at a different location. I have an expense account that even pays for drinks with lunch. Or, we can skip lunch and start with happy hour?"

"Does she speak English?" Laura asked from behind Russ.

"I speak it. I write it. And I televise it," Galassi said from the doorway.

"Sorry. Not this time," Russ said. "If you'll take just one little step back . . ."

She stepped back.

". . . I'll close this door," he said.

The door slammed in front of the obnoxious woman.

"Careful with the door slamming," Esther said. "You'd hate to burst her Botox."

Russ received four or five more phone messages from the woman during the next month. He never got around to returning the calls.

"HAVE YOU got a minute?" Detective Pfeifer asked his partner.

"Let me get my coffee," Leonard Roberts said. "You want some?"

Pfeifer nodded and waited while Detective Roberts went to the break room and returned with two cups of strong black coffee. Roberts put Pfeifer's coffee on the desk blotter and balanced himself against the edge of the wooden desk.

"You've got that look on your face that makes me think you've been thinking too much," he said to Pfeifer.

"Could be. What if there truly was a get-away car out front the day of Laura Howard's bank robbery?"

"She'll slap you silly if she hears you call it *her* robbery."

"Semantics," Pfeifer said.

"You really want to resurrect the black Scion? We spent every spare minute we had on that for days and didn't turn up anything."

"True. But, now we have Laura Howard run off the road by what bystanders and other drivers describe as a small black car," Pfeifer said.

"Did even one of them say 'Scion?'"

"No. But, the incident was after dark."

"True."

"And they wouldn't have known we'd been on the lookout for that car."

175

"Plus this latest incident would follow the pattern of a criminal getting more brazen with each crime. First he drives a getaway car. That's just a notch above 'aiding and abetting.' Then he moves on to stalking and vandalism, followed by threatening the woman in her own kitchen. Not looking good," Roberts added.

"Yep," Pfeifer said. "And once he figures out that Laura Howard is no fool, and he's not going to silence her by defacing her garden and threatening her face to face, he amps it up by running her off the road."

"Damn. I hate it when you're right."

"Raising the canopy of the trees surrounding your house lets light into the rooms. It also deters potential burglars."

22

The white and green business card was tucked between the heavy carved wood front door and the door hinges at The Harrington. Laura had no idea how long the card had been there. It wasn't weathered and she doubted that she could have missed seeing it when she left earlier this morning.

The card offered general landscaping service and scheduled weekly lawn and yard care, plus promised reasonable rates. She glanced outside at the remains of the parkway strip in front of her house and wondered if she was the only resident to receive the calling card or if someone had walked the length of the block advertising yard care services to all.

She flipped the card over in her hand and had the answer. "I noticed your yard when I was driving by. Rolando."

I'll bet you did, she thought. Her yard was pretty much one-of-a-kind compared to the other nicely groomed landscaped plots on the block. It wouldn't hurt to call whoever left the card and ask for some references. It would make her feel more at ease to know that others in the area approved of "Rolando's" services. The front of the card was more formal. Rolando Perez Yard Service was printed in caps and lower case letters above business license and phone numbers.

Several of Laura's neighbors claimed to have seen Rolando's truck on streets nearby, but all of them said they either preferred to do their own yard work or already had other yard help so hadn't called him. The yards he groomed looked good, they all agreed.

Laura admired anyone who was industrious in searching out new clients. And, she wanted the yard in perfect order for Esther and Ernie's big day. She admitted to herself that she'd spent more time lately thinking about herself than the coming nuptials. But, there was still time before their wedding day. She'd call the gardener, ask for references, and, if those rang true, she'd start by hiring him for a two-week trial period.

Rolando was a wiry young man of average height. He had a quick smile and warm brown eyes. None of which told Laura how well he did yard work, she thought. But, she hired him anyway. It wasn't as if she was inviting a stranger inside The Harrington. Rolando would come and go on his own schedule, bring all his own tools, and bill monthly. And, she thought, save my sanity while I concentrate on plans for the approaching Gallo-Graham nuptials.

WHEN THE NEW gardener arrived to restore the parkway and plant the replacement tree, Laura knew she'd made the right decision. Mr. Perez worked like no gardener she'd ever watched. He was busy every minute that he was there and he hustled from the front to the back of the house at a quick clip, tidying up the flower beds all around. He was in constant motion, checking the back, front, and each side of the house.

He must have done manual labor most of his life, Laura thought, as she watched him through the living room window. He effortlessly lifted the crape myrtle tree she'd chosen from the city's list of approved parkway trees. He balanced the tree in the hole he'd readied and carefully added the soil around the base of the trunk.

According to the website she had consulted, the berries on this tree were supposed to attract birds. Laura thought Louise might enjoy watching the birds through the front windows.

As good a reason to choose a tree as any other, she thought. The tree was also not expected to grow to a height that would overpower the house. If she could believe whichever city panel approved the tree . . .

Rolando finished the job by supporting the tree with cotton ropes he'd placed inside sections of rubber hose to avoid damaging the trunk. Then, he was back at her front door.

He'd been working hard and sweat rolled down his face from under his floppy straw hat. It was one of the first bright sunny days this spring. Laura had a similar hat she'd retrieved from the backyard gardening shed at The Harrington. She wore hers to prevent freckles from forming across the bridge of her nose. She suspected he donned his as a jaunty fashion statement.

"I've got a flat of periwinkle left over from another job," he said. "If you like, I can plant it around the base of the tree. No charge. It has glossy leaves and blue and purple color in spring. Having it there would help the water soak in around the new tree."

"Do periwinkles attract slugs?" she asked.

"Oregon slugs aren't selective. They eat *everything*."

"I've noticed."

She'd followed Rolando's advice earlier not to choose a maple tree because of a current pest outbreak that gardeners feared might spread and decrease the tree canopy in the city. Who knew? If Rolando thought periwinkle would look good beneath the tree, it was fine with her. Future slugs and all.

She stood back to admire his work.

"Right tree, right place," he assured her as he looked at the groundcover around the base of the tree and repeated instructions on watering. They both glanced at the darkening sky and decided she could delay watering if the approaching storm materialized.

After his third visit, Laura interrupted Rolando's work to ask for a statement for his services.

"You're not happy with the work?" he asked.

"I'm extremely happy," she said. "But, I need to pay you for what you've done so far."

"So, I'm not fired?"

"Of course not," she said. "The yard has never looked better."

The man seemed relieved and promised to bring a statement with him when he returned,

She heard Rolando working outside three more times during the following week. Plus, he'd made brief stops at the house to use a leaf blower along the sidewalks in front of the house on days he wasn't scheduled to be there. It wasn't a service she requested, but, if it all came in the monthly fee he had quoted, she had no complaint.

"Bottom line," Laura told Esther. "My sore ribs won't let me bend and stretch to do yard work right now. And, my front yard has never looked better."

"WHAT DO YOU know about the gardener Laura hired?" Russ asked Esther.

"He seems nice enough. I assumed *you* checked him out."

"Not yet, but I'm about to do just that. I think Chris Pfeifer will understand our concern."

"What's this 'our' stuff? I liked Rolando the minute I met him," Esther fired back.

"I know he's charming. That's not the issue. I need to know that he's also not an ex-con," Russ said.

"Suit yourself."

Russ decided no time was better than now. He called Pfeifer from his truck as he drove through town.

"Why don't you meet me for a cup of coffee at the Denny's Restaurant in the shopping center down by your place? Ten o'clock?" Pfeifer asked.

"Got it."

Russ watched Pfeifer swing the unmarked car easily into the restaurant parking lot. They each got out of vehicles and entered the restaurant where they took a seat away from the other occupied tables. They ordered coffee and a piece of pie each. Oregon marionberry for Pfeifer. Apple for Russ.

"I appreciate your concern," the detective said while they waited for the pie. "I probably should have alerted you, but it's one of those situations where we get stuck between using common sense and following policy."

"How so?" Russ asked.

"The gardener works for us."

Russ had taken a gulp of hot coffee, and choked it back into the cup when he heard the response. "You're kidding me," he said.

"This is absolutely between you and me," Pfeifer said. "When Rolando Hernandez isn't at Laura's tending her plants, he and his partner have her house under surveillance, circling the neighborhood a few times a day and most of the night."

"Her landscaper's a cop?" Russ asked quietly. "I thought his name was 'Perez.'"

"It is to Laura."

"She told me she got his name from a business card stuck in her door," Russ added.

"He was hand-selected for this assignment," Pfeifer said. "He and his wife keep the yard in their little rental house like a park. They've got one kid and another one on the way."

"And Laura went for this?"

"We didn't tell her and I'm trusting that you won't either."

"Absolutely not," Russ said. "When I saw the guy out there on a sunny day last week, I thought he was Laura taking her aggression out on those poor weeds along the side of the drive."

"We know Ms. Howard pretty well by now," Pfeifer said. "We figured there's no way she would agree to twenty-four-hour surveillance. If the business card gambit hadn't worked, we'd have figured out something else."

Russ thanked the man and picked up the tab.

"Cactus gardens are the perfect oxymoron."

23

Pfeifer checked in at the end of his shift and headed across the parking lot to his car. He moved through traffic easily and landed the vehicle at the Red Robin restaurant. He ordered his usual "sautéed 'shroom burger" and tower of onion rings. He sat in a back upholstered booth away from the lounge area, quietly enjoying his meal and rehashing the events since the bank robbery.

It didn't seem fair that the reward for a citizen attempting to stop a bank robbery should be a life full of harassment and threats. But, then, the world wasn't always fair. He'd learned that during the first six months as a police officer. He toyed with the onion tower and thought about the investigatory steps they'd taken so far.

Two rookie officers had been assigned to go door-to-door in Laura Howard's neighborhood after the rock had been hurled through the front window of her house. They turned up nothing. The rest of the neighbors had slept right through the event.

If the driver at the bank that day thought that he'd been seen and that Laura could identify him. . . Pfeifer let his mind wander. Would that be enough reason to vandalize her house and later wave a gun at her at The Harrington?

And, he wondered, who names a house?

He'd grown to respect Russell Graham. He hoped the man was aware of the responsibility he'd taken on when he'd first hired the decorator.

Pfeifer and Leonard Roberts had formed a solid investigative team, but this time they disagreed. Roberts wasn't buying Laura's report of a Scion get-away car. Pfeifer believed her. If the woman said she saw a Scion, she probably did. She'd been scared at the bank that day, but she hadn't been blinded.

"Recovering outdated upholstered furniture is like putting a tutu on a hippo."

24

Esther offered to take Hammer for his morning walk. It was one of those wonderful but rare sunny days in late February in Portland. Both Esther and Hammer longed to be outside enjoying the pre-spring day.

"Go get your leash," she said to the dog. Hammer left and returned from Russ' office with the red leather leash in his mouth.

"Good boy."

Esther trotted down the block, trying to keep up with the large dog. To casual observers it was difficult to tell who was walking whom. Esther enjoyed the warm sun on her back. Hammer was more interested in checking out every tree trunk along the route and the occasional fire hydrant. As they neared Laura's house on the return trip, Esther noticed Rolando's truck was out front, but she didn't see the gardener.

187

Esther was impressed by the man's work ethic. Had she been the gardener, she'd have been tempted to play hooky today and sit in one of the yard chairs behind Laura's house, enjoying the unseasonal sunshine.

Hammer noticed none of this, but hadn't missed one fire hydrant.

Rolando came down the driveway carrying a leaf blower. Esther hated those tools, but chose to keep her opinion quiet and introduced herself to Rolando. They visited for a few minutes before Rolando pulled out a wallet and showed Esther a photo of his toddler son Diego. The man was bursting with pride and Esther raved about how much father and son resembled each other and then went on down the block with Hammer.

"WHATEVER YOU'RE paying your new yard guy," Esther told Laura when she returned to Graham Construction and freed Hammer from his leash, "it's worth every penny. That yard's never looked so good."

"Thanks. I'll tell him you said so."

"I already did."

Laura heard the sirens going past the office and was relieved that, for once, the squad cars hadn't been dispatched in response to a 911 call from her. She longed for the quiet life that she'd established for a short while before going to the bank that morning two months ago.

Five minutes later there was pounding on the side door at Graham Construction.

"Police," a deep male voice yelled.

Russ opened the door. "May I help you?"

"I was told by a neighbor that I might find a Ms. Laura Howard here," the officer said.

"Laura's here." He turned and called to Laura to join him at the door. "Is there trouble, officer?"

"May I come in?"

"Of course," Laura said from behind Russ. "Why do I suspect this isn't a social call?"

"I think we'd better sit down if that's all right with you," the man said. Laura hadn't seen this particular officer when she'd been in and out of the police bureau these past two months. She chided herself silently about how familiar she had become with the local police and their procedures. It definitely wasn't how she had pictured her adult life would be when she was a daydreaming teenager.

They moved the few feet to the work table where Esther was already seated.

"There's been an emergency up the block," he said. "The neighbor who reported what appears to be a crime scene said that we could find Ms. Howard here."

Laura took a deep breath. "That's me."

189

Russ entered the room. "Officer, can you tell us what's happened?" he asked.

"There's been a fatality. We thought at first that we might have had a stroke or heart attack victim. It looked like the man had stretched across the driveway to weed along the edges of the cement, but, on closer inspection, we found the victim had been shot."

Laura paled.

The cop looked down to check his notes. "The man who found him, a Mr. Gargenzio, says he may have seen the victim at Ms. Howard's place earlier this week doing yard work."

Laura gasped and put her head in her hands. "Rolando," she said quietly.

Russ put his arm across her shoulders and pulled her toward him.

"Who's Rolando?" the officer asked.

"The yard man," Esther said. "I just talked with him this morning. Maybe fifteen minutes ago. Did it look like he was shot at the location where Gargenzio found him?" Esther asked.

"We suspect so. We haven't taken time to look for evidence yet that indicates that the body had been deposited there after death. Why would you ask that?"

"Just curious," she said. "Could the shooter have had the wrong house? That happened to me in this block."

Laura marveled at how calm and rational Esther could stay in situations like this. .

"Mrs. Graham, you ask some interesting questions" the officer said.

"I was an emergency room nurse."

"Ms. Howard," the officer said. "I know this is a shock to you, but we need to know how to reach the next of kin for the victim. Then, eventually, we'll need to talk to you about your employer-employee relationship with the deceased."

"Of course."

"For a start, what was the victim's full name?"

"Rolando Perez," she said.

"Not exactly," Russ said.

Laura looked surprised. "What do you mean by 'not exactly.'?"

"Officer," he said. He hesitated for a few seconds. "Officer, this may be upsetting to both you and Laura. The 'yard man' was named Rolando Hernandez and he worked for the Portland Police Bureau."

Laura looked stunned. The officer didn't register any recognition of the name Russ had given him.

"You can call Detectives Christopher Pfeifer or Leonard Roberts for details," Russ said.

Laura recovered enough to remember that she had Pfeifer's business card in her purse, pulled it out, and handed it to the man. She thought later that he probably knew the number for his own place of work.

RUSS SEEMED almost as shaken as Laura when the officer left. Esther bustled around the small kitchen with make-shift work to give the two of them some time to digest the news.

"You knew?" Laura asked Russ.

"Not initially," Russ said. "I was concerned about you hiring a man simply because you found his business card in your door. I asked Pfeifer to check him out."

"I'd done a reference check already," Laura said.

"Pfeifer's reference check was a little more thorough. He told me that Rolando 'Perez' was actually Rolando Hernandez, an undercover officer they had assigned to keep your house under surveillance until they could apprehend whoever tried to kill you by running you off the road."

"And you didn't tell me?"

"We both know how you would have reacted," he said.

Russ picked up his cell phone on the first ring. He listened intently, said "I'll tell her," and hung up.

"That was Roberts. He sounded a little shook. He and Pfeifer are on their way over here."

"Natural straw baskets placed on bookcase shelves are God's answer to clutter."

25

"Ms. Howard, you need to get out of town. Now," Roberts said. "We failed to protect you once. It's too risky for you to stay in Portland now."

"Today?" Laura asked.

"This minute."

Laura, Esther and Detectives Roberts and Pfeifer were standing on the front porch at The Harrington.

"Can I take Esther with me?"

"We'll get you two a car."

Esther perked up. "A cruiser?"

"An older non-descript sedan," he answered. "No siren."

"You've got twenty minutes to get packed for wherever you decide to go. Don't tell anyone, but . . ."

He hesitated to look around the group. "Don't tell anyone but Detective Pfeifer where you're heading. He'll give you a phone you can use to contact him. Only him."

"Not me. Not Russell Graham. No one but Pfeifer. Have you got that?" he asked. "Graham will have to understand. We're not taking any chances until we get whoever this is in custody."

This protective side of Roberts was new to Laura. He was still all business, but there was warmth and concern in his voice.

As soon as Roberts was through giving orders, Pfeifer took over. He instructed Laura and Esther to meet him at the church on the corner near The Harrington in twenty minutes. He'd be driving their "new ride" and swap them for Esther's Element on the scene, he explained. He and only he would know their destination, he stressed.

"You'll have surveillance," he said simply. "You've fifteen minutes to pack and then to decide where you're going. You're smart ladies. Think of somewhere the creep who shot Rolando won't think to look for you."

He turned to two officers on the scene and asked them to follow the women into their homes while they packed. Laura did a quick calculation and realized they'd have less than five minutes on the drive to the church to agree on a destination.

Esther saw the strained look on Laura's face. "No worry," she said. "I've got this one."

Laura was glad to hear that because the first place that came to her mind was Wyoming and she didn't know how to get there other than to point the loaner car southeast and step on the gas. She also thought that destination might be a bit extreme.

"My mind going off course again," she muttered. "Get a grip," she told herself. She'd definitely let Esther decide on their destination.

THEY LOOKED past Pfeifer's car the first time they rounded the corner. On their second trip around the block in Esther's vehicle, they spotted a ten-year-old Ford Taurus with a single occupant. The beige sedan blended in with the row of parked cars and the buildings behind it. Pfeifer was good. He'd found "non-descript" in spades.

When he got out of the car he was wearing jeans and a sweatshirt and a stocking cap. He flipped the key chain toward Esther without a word. As Laura walked past him toward the passenger side door, he took off the hat and handed it to her. "Wear it," he said. And he was gone.

The women didn't speak until they were approaching the Interstate 5 on-ramp.

"I'm not sure the hat will help that much," Laura said. "Besides, it's too big for me. I have a straw gardening hat at home that's identical to the one Rolando was wearing."

"Think about that," Esther told her.

Laura was quiet.

"Wake up!" Esther said and snapped her fingers. "The shooter thought Rolando was you in the yard at The Harrington."

"You truly believe that?"

"Why did you think Roberts went into action so quickly?"

"I didn't think."

"Well, snap to, "Esther said.

"I'm in real danger this time."

""What do you mean 'this time,' *kemosabe*?"

Laura looked blank. She was too young to remember The Lone Ranger's Indian friend and silver bullets, and Esther was concentrating on maneuvering through traffic in Portland and didn't take time to explain.

"WE'RE THE ONLY ones in the car," Laura said to driver Esther. "Don't you think you can tell me where we're going?"

"The Oregon coast," Esther answered simply. "And, we're not alone," she said surveying the backed up traffic on the interstate.

"Shouldn't we be headed west on US 26?"

"That's precisely what the idiot who shot Rolando would expect," Esther said. "I've got this under control. Just sit back and relax."

Esther shot across two lanes to get to the far left lane and put her foot on the gas pedal. Laura doubted she could follow the command to relax while Esther was at the wheel.

"What do you mean we're not alone?" She glanced behind her for the first time and saw the cat carrier wedged between the back and front seats on the floor on the driver's side. "Louise?"

The cat yowled back.

"Now you've done it," Esther said. "Rummage through the front compartments of the car and see if you can find any CD's to play to drown out that beast. "

When Laura couldn't turn up any country artists, Esther settled for an old Grateful Dead selection.

Neither of them spoke again until south of Salem when Laura questioned the route again.

"We're going to cut over at Albany," Esther said. "Then we'll take Highway 20 through Corvallis and Philomath. Then, we'll cut off at Highway 34."

"And, that will take us where?" Laura asked.

"With your weak stomach, probably to the side of the road," Esther responded. "Highway 20 is less windy, but there's less traffic on 34 and no one would expect us to choose the curvier route."

"And, we land where?"

"You'll see."

"When did you have time to put Louise in the car?" she asked.

"Not me. Detective Roberts remembered him."

ESTHER HADN'T been kidding when she'd described the winding two-lane state route. Laura alternated between the urge to be carsick and the one to scream as Esther wound the unfamiliar car quickly through the curvy road that cut through the tall trees.

"Why don't you try to sleep?" Esther suggested.

"I couldn't possibly."

Laura suspected her reply offended Esther. There was no more conversation in the car until the road straightened and they saw the bay on the right of the road. The sign said they were approaching Waldport, and Laura said a silent prayer that this was their destination.

The cat had sulked in his carrier in the back seat of the car since they'd passed Alsea high school's Wolverine marching band practicing on the field to the left of the highway.

When they reached Waldport, Esther had a choice of going straight (and into the surf) or turning north or south at the first signal light. Laura gasped when Esther signaled right, then hung a left, and headed south.

"Was someone behind us?" Laura asked.

"Nope. I just always wanted to do that," Esther said. "It's a weekday, early evening. We're not going to find much traffic from here on out."

Laura recognized that they had landed on Hwy. 101. A light fog was blowing across the highway as the skies darkened.

"Where do you plan to land this thing?" she asked.

"Patience," Esther advised. "You'll see."

Laura sat back, trying to get glimpses of the ocean to her right and a series of tattered beach cottages mixed with "new builds" to her left. Esther had predicted correctly. The traffic grew sparser as the sky darkened.

Without reaching for the turn signal lever, Esther made a quick turn. She pulled into a wide parking lot with a long, low motel building on the west side of the highway. A series of poorly painted doors, lined up like dominos, faced the parking area.

"Welcome to ..."

"The Bates Motel?" Laura interrupted. "This place looks deserted. And creepy."

"I was going to say 'Yachats—where the pines meet the palms.' If I'd thought we needed elegance, I'd have chosen The Adobe or The Fireside. This time we want to go unnoticed. This'll be fine."

Laura was skeptical. "If you say so," she said.

"Louise will be welcome here, too," Esther added.

"No doubt," Laura said glancing at the weathered neon motel sign.

After checking that the car doors were locked, Laura followed Esther to the motel office to sign in at their temporary lodgings. Very temporary, she hoped.

Esther then moved the car to the south side of the building. Pfeifer couldn't have picked a better car to blend into the foggy surroundings, she thought. Laura lifted the cat carrier from the backseat and Esther removed their two small bags of clothing from the car trunk, slammed the trunk lid, and headed across the row of motel room doors.

Esther held the key to Room 8, located about two-thirds of the way down the strip. She looked both ways before inserting the key. The lock clicked promisingly and Esther pushed the door open. They scooted through the doorway into the darkened room, closing the door behind them and securing the chain lock.

"It'll be just fine once we get the drapes open," Esther said.

And, to Laura's relief, it was. The room was clean and looked out on the ocean. Or would if the fog lifted in the morning. It would provide the "cover" they needed until they got the signal from Pfeifer that it was safe to return. The simple room had both front and back exits which Laura inspected twice to make sure the doors were locked and the heavy chain locks in place.

"Do you think the desk man knew that wasn't my real name?" Laura asked.

"Of course he did," Esther said. "Who signs in as Ellen Hide?"

"It wasn't my brightest move," Laura admitted. "I've always liked the name Ellen. After it was out of my mouth all I could think of was Ellen Degeneres. And, she's a blonde."

"And?" Esther asked.

"She can dance," Laura said. "What name did you use?"

"Esther Pfeifer."

"Esther Pfeifer? Say it fast and it sounds like a sneeze. *Estherpfeifer!*"

"Geshundheit!"

"Thank you," Laura said, "I spelled my new last name with a 'y.' Ellen Hyde."

"Yeah. Like that'll help."

"You should talk. Who uses a cop's name?" Laura asked.

"Anyone who remembers that the cop secured the room for us on his personal credit card before we left Portland."

"Bed sheets are like saltines. They should be crisp and white."

26

If he'd wanted to be a beat cop, Pfeifer thought, he wouldn't have taken all that college course work to qualify to interview for the detective's job.

He could have asked someone else on the force to walk the area where Laura Howard lived, but his colleagues were still reeling from Rolando Hernandez' death. There wasn't much conversation about the death, but Pfeifer could tell by the strain on the faces of the men and women coming in and out of the Bureau. They had all contributed generously to a fund set up for his wife and children.

Several squad members had stepped forward to be pall bearers at the service which was covered heavily by local television stations. Local newspapers editorialized about a growing trend of violence against police officers and a separate memorial fund was set up so community members could contribute funds to build a permanent memorial to honor Hernandez.

Now, Pfeifer walked three blocks north and two blocks south of Laura Howard's home, stepping up to the front entry of each home. No one yet, including the Neighborhood Watch crew members, had seen anything out of the ordinary in the past two days.

He crossed the street and reversed direction, again passing The Harrington. No one was home at the first five houses. The older woman at the next house, who elected to explain at length why she hadn't joined the Neighborhood Watch Group, hadn't seen or heard anything out of the ordinary. She reminisced about going to the policemen's ball when she was a child, and wanted to know why those events were no longer held.

Detective Pfeifer gave her the phone number for the Community Policing division so he could escape from her front porch. He knew they'd be diplomatic in answering her questions.

At the next house, he hit pay dirt. An attractive older woman came to the door. He introduced himself, showed his identification, and asked her the same set of questions.

"Have you noticed any unusual activity in the area lately? Any strangers walking past? Any cars that didn't belong to the residents?" Pfeifer hesitated to catch his breath.

"I'm a member of the Neighborhood Watch Group," she said. "So I'm well aware of what to watch for around here."

Pfeifer sighed. Each time he'd roused a member of the Watch group today, it had taken him ten minutes extra to break free and continue up the block.

"I have my chalkboard right here," she said, reaching toward her right. She stepped out the front door onto the covered porch with him and thrust a 12 x 12 inch child's chalk board at him.

There were seven different license plate numbers written down. All Oregon plates.

"Here," she said. "This one never returned," she said and pointed at a license plate number written on the board in chalk. "I give it two weeks, though, before I erase the plate numbers."

"Wise," he said.

"This one always comes at dusk. I've seen it four times, but I only got the plate number written down three of those times."

Pfeifer perked up. He thought he recognized the license plate numbers listed to the left of the board. Then he realized it was the plate of the undercover car

Rolando Hernandez was issued while he was assigned to protect Laura Howard.

"You're right on top of things," he said.

"There's no point gong to the Watch meetings if you're not going to follow through on your own time when you get home. Don't you think?"

"Definitely," he said. "What can you tell me about this set of numbers?" he asked about the last list of license plate numbers.

"I've seen that license three times. I wrote it down twice around four in the afternoon and one time closer to bedtime. The license plate is a little crumpled on the lower right side and my eyes aren't so good anymore. That's why I have the number listed the same twice and then listed a third time with a different last number. It's hard to tell if that third number's a three or an eight."

"Would you mind if I copy these down?"

"Not at all. Why don't you step inside?"

PFEIFER COMPLETED his rounds, but no one else supplied any useful information. Sally Emerson, the resident who had done her homework on the chalkboard, had provided the only lead. He'd take the numbers back to the Bureau and check them out.

He couldn't wait to tell the undercover guys that their car had been made by an elderly lady with limited eyesight.

That could wait. He was on his own time while surveying the neighborhood and was ready to head home. Wouldn't it be something if the old schoolhouse chalkboard beat out all the computer searches they had tried down at headquarters?

"Blackboard paint is great for a small area in a child's room, but don't overdo it. Those kids need to be out playing in the sunshine, not perfecting their graffiti skills."

27

"Got him!" he said under his breath.

Chris Pfeifer had stayed late at the Police Bureau to follow up on the license plate numbers Mrs. Emerson had provided. The first plate she reported was issued to a car that now sat in a junk yard after the driver's insurance company had declared it "totaled."

There was no point in double checking the plate on the police surveillance vehicle.

The third one showing on the computer screen, the car with the plate ending in the number eight, was registered to an owner with a Burnside area address.

Pfeifer fought against falling into the trap of labeling someone as a potential suspect because he lived in a less prosperous part of town. But, several years as a cop told him that an apartment house in lower Burnside was a more likely address for a criminal than the expensive houses on river view roads with three and four car garages.

Unless the car had changed hands since it was last registered, it belonged to a small-time crook. Mickey Crump, d.o.b. 9-27-81, male, Caucasian.

"Burglary, assault, arson, possession of narcotics (methamphetamine), obstruction of justice, tampering with a witness, breaking and entering. . ." he read from the computer screen.

Add the charges from the other night in the kitchen at The Harrington, get a conviction, and this guy is toast, Pfeifer thought.

If he were a newbie officer, Pfeifer would wonder why the suspect was still out on the street. But, Chris Pfeifer had been around long enough to know some of these "habituals" were in and out of custody in less time than it took his uniform shirt to be cleaned for his next shift.

Now Pfeifer wondered if the suspect was warped enough to carry out a drive by shooting. The autopsy results of Rolando Hernandez' death had been released earlier today. The examiners concluded that the shot was fired from a distance of approximately thirty feet. That was also the distance between where the body fell and the skid marks in the street.

Pfeifer needed to act quickly to put out an APB to get this guy off the street and into a lineup where Laura Howard could identify him. Or maybe not. Sometimes witnesses could be so traumatized that everyone in the lineup looked dangerous, and no one stood out.

Pfeifer suspected, though, that Laura Howard had enough grit not to let panic set in. He hoped so anyway. If Mr. Crump was guilty of driving the get-away car at the bank and breaking into Laura's house and holding her at gunpoint, he'd be residing in a cell even smaller than a wrong-side-of-town apartment.

And those charges didn't include "vehicular assault on a truck," a phony charge Pfeifer planned to tell Laura he had filed. He knew how much she loved that truck.

Having a name for the suspect excited Pfeifer. He wanted to get this guy. Badly.

My last girlfriend might have been right when she delivered her exit line, Pfeifer thought. Maybe he would always be married to his job, but it was a solid, happy marriage and it beat the heck out of many of the marriages he had seen.

If in doubt, delay monogramming the towels until after your first wedding anniversary."

28

Laura peeked through the windows to enjoy the ocean view when she woke on the fourth day of their exile. The trip had moved from vacation status to exile status late last night. She missed Portland. She missed her house. And, every inch of the motel room smelled like Louise's cat food dish.

"I need fresh air," she moaned.

"Not a problem," Esther said. "Just let me call Pete and Jamie first."

"Pete and Jamie? We don't know a Pete and Jamie."

"But, they know us," Esther explained. "The two of them and have been with us since we left the church in Portland."

"You're kidding me."

"No. Pfeifer and I decided not to tell you before we left so you wouldn't freak out."

"Freak out!" Laura yelled.

"Example Number eighty-seven," Esther said.

"I'm not freaking out because you left me in the dark on this. That's just part of it," she said. "I don't think I'll ever get over the guilt that Rolando was killed because of me. Now, two additional officers are assigned the same job. How does that make sense?"

"I had planned to tell you all along," Esther said. "Pfeifer's worried about how much more stress you can take. He made me promise to tell you once we got settled in over here."

"And you're just now getting around to it?"

"It took until today for me to feel 'settled in,'" Esther said. "Do you want to have breakfast out?" she asked to change the subject. "There's The Green Salmon Coffee Shop or, if you want a more traditional breakfast, we can always try Leroy's Blue Whale."

"How do you know all this?"

"Keep it under your hat, but Ernie and I have spent more than a couple of weekends together over here. There are enough restaurants in the little town that we shouldn't have to repeat until Day Six."

"Please tell me there won't be a Day Six?" Laura said. "I'm running out of clothes and I didn't bring anything to read."

They drove the few miles to what Esther insisted on calling "Greater Yachats" in spite of the population sign that listed 703 residents.

RUSS CONTACTED Pfeifer to make sure the women had arrived safely. He didn't need nor want to know their exact location, but knew he wouldn't relax until he heard from Pfeifer that they were alive and well wherever they were.

Pfeifer then called Pete and Jamie and reminded them to be vigilant about their own safety in addition to that of the two women. There hadn't been an official determination yet on whether Hernandez had been the planned target, whether Laura was the intended victim, or whether a deranged shooter was randomly taking out police officers.

PFEIFER MET Russ again at the neighborhood Denny's for a cup of coffee and so Russ could again thank Pfeifer for getting Laura out of town and to a safe location. During the conversation, Pfeifer pointed out that Laura might need someone to protect her full time even after the current threat ended.

"Don't let her hear that," Russ said.

"I'm not that dumb. I know spunky when I meet spunky," he added. "There was a time a couple of years ago when I would have competed with you for that job, but not now."

"You know, I've asked her to marry me," Russ said.

"And?"

"We don't have a date set."

"Congratulations, anyway," Pfeifer said. "As I said, I was definitely interested in our Ms. Howard at one time. Since then, I decided I'd never expose a woman to the perils of being married to a cop. Rolando's death re-affirmed that."

"I'll do my best to take care of her."

"You damned well better," Pfeifer said.

DO YOU REALIZE," Laura asked from her deck chair in the sun, "that I may have had crackers and peanut butter in my Portland kitchen with a murderer?"

"*You* didn't realize that earlier?" Esther asked.

"I might have, but I try not to dwell on the negative. The thought just resurfaced."

"Well, Pete and Whatshisname are well aware of it and they'll make sure there's no repeat performance at the coast. You want to sit in the sun or go buy a book?"

"Both."

It was not unusual to have unseasonably warm weather at the coast for a few days in February. The locals knew it was a "fake out" and not the signal that winter was over.

There were weathered Adirondack chairs on the back deck. A row of ice plants at the edge of the deck and cacti planted in half wine barrels were reminiscent of 1967 gardening trends.

Esther phoned their body guards and reported that she and Laura would be en route to the bookstore in ten minutes and then drive north on Hwy 101 to Outta-Gas Pizza for a cheeseburger. They'd had the pizza last night. Esther favored The Drift Inn, a favorite pub of Ernie's, but she wasn't sure she'd get the OK from Pete. The place had good food, good music, but too many entrances.

"Where am I going to find a book in a town this size?" Laura asked. "I doubt anyone here can compete with Barnes and Nobel or Powell's Bookstore here."

"You don't need those big bruisers. Yachats has Mari's Books, the sweetest little bookstore in the state. It's no bigger than your living room at The Harrington, but it has everything you need in a bookstore," Esther said. "The atmosphere, the smell of books, the selection. Trust me. If word ever gets out about Mari's, Lincoln

County will have to put in an airstrip here. The place is that good."

LAURA LEFT the bookstore with several used paperback mysteries and one nearly-new biography. She figured those would last her until she and Esther could return to Portland. They wandered along the blacktop walkway to the grocery store on the same strip with Mari's Books.

Laura had confessed earlier to growing uneasy each time they passed a green and white tsunami warning sign. Esther explained when they saw the first one that seeing a "tsunami zone" warning sign and actually experiencing a tsunami were two different things.

"What would we do if we did hear a warning?" Laura had asked.

"Don't ask questions and run like H up the other side of the highway."

"And?"

"Don't stop running," Esther added.

ESTHER SELECTED sweet rolls, candy bars, and a tin of peanuts to add to the grocery cart. Laura chose apples, oranges, a box of Wheat Thins and cheese. They wound through the narrow aisles and back up to the cashier.

They unloaded their snacks and the items moved automatically toward the cashier, but the employee stood absolutely still, staring at Laura. He didn't reach for the groceries.

"You OK?" Esther asked him.

"Yes, of course. Sorry, it's just odd is all," he said.

"What's odd?"

"Your friend," he said looking at Laura. "A man was in here a little over an hour ago with a picture asking if I'd seen anyone who looked like the photo. I'd swear the photo was of you," he said to Laura. "The photo looked like it'd been taken off a TV screen."

"What did you tell him?" Laura asked.

"Nothing," he said. "I hadn't seen you yet. And, even if I had, I probably wouldn't have told the man anything. He was a scruffy looking guy. Probably in his sixties, unshaven, out of shape."

"So, he didn't look like a police officer?" Laura asked.

"About as far from that as you can get."

Esther threw a twenty dollar bill on the counter. "He's her abusive 'ex,'" she told the grocery clerk.

The two women grabbed their un-bagged purchases and scooted out the front door.

"Thanks," Laura called out to the cashier.

The clerk shook his head. Why would a woman who looked like Laura have married a guy like that in the first place?

"So what now?" Laura asked as they closed and locked the doors on the Taurus.

"We assume he didn't get any information. We drive back to the motel. Lock the door and call Pfeifer."

"And?"

"That's all I've got," Esther said. "I'm making this up as I go."

"The description doesn't match the man who was in my kitchen," Laura said.

"Not Bernie or Clyde either."

"I've about had it up to here," Laura said. "Why wouldn't the police tailing us have seen this guy?"

"Call me crazy," Esther said, "but I'd say it was because they're guarding us and didn't get to the grocery store until we did."

"Point taken," Laura said. "I'll give 'em a pass this time."

Laura's cell phone was ringing as they stepped into the motel room. Pfeifer was calling to alert them that he'd had a call from the Multnomah County Sheriff's office reporting that one of their deputies had ticketed one Mickey Crump twenty minutes before their department had received an all-points bulletin alerting other agencies that Crump was sought for questioning by the Portland Police Bureau.

"Precisely what time was he in Portland?" Laura asked.

"The ticket was issued at 1:04 p.m. and our bulletin went out at 1:30. Why do you ask?"

Laura looked at her watch.

"It's only 2:15 now. So, there's no way he could be at the coast already?"

"Impossible," Pfeifer said. "What's going on?"

"When I was at the grocery store a bit ago, the clerk said someone had been there showing my photo and asking if I'd been seen in the store."

"Damn."

"My thought exactly," Laura said.

"Where are you now?"

"Back at the motel, locked in the room. I was going to tell Pete and Jamie when your call came in," she added.

"I'll do that," Pfeifer said. "You stay put. Get the drapes drawn if they're not already."

Laura repeated Pfeifer's message to Esther who decided this was suddenly a two-candy-bar occasion.

"Two each," she clarified as she distributed the Snickers Bars.

"Thrown Mexican pottery can cause injuries to cheating spouses."

29

Esther's cell phone rang.

"Your motel over there just experienced a boom in business," caller Pfeifer told her. "Pete's in the adjoining room to the south and Jamie has Room 9. One of them will pick up dinner for the four of you. You two stay put."

She barely had time to say "thanks" before the line went dead.

PFEIFER SENSED a new urgency in getting to the bottom of the threats against Laura Howard. Late this morning, he had turned to another detective in the Bureau for help verifying that Crump still lived at the address of record. That colleague uncovered a second, more recent address for Crump. A run-down triplex on the other side of the Sellwood Bridge.

They now had an eye-witness description of Crump. They knew what he was driving, and now they had an up-to-date address. Why was the suspect still at large?

As he pondered the information they had collected, a report of an injury accident on Martin Luther King Jr. Blvd. popped up on his computer screen.

A local woman driving a late model BMW had been crossing the intersection with the signal light in her favor when an older model car blew through a red light and careened into her vehicle. That second car was a Scion, which then ricocheted into a police cruiser.

Pfeifer instantly called to put a hold on the driver of the Scion. They'd have to wait until the man was treated for his injuries, the officers on scene told Pfeifer, but they'd see that he was released to the police and no one else.

He ended the call and turned toward Roberts. "Sometimes we solve 'em," he told the detective seated across the room. "And sometimes the suspects fall right in our lap."

After more details about the accident came in, he updated Roberts.

"I'd gotten a new address for the guy who we suspect held Laura Howard at gunpoint in her kitchen. I was sitting here compiling info from his rap sheet when a call came in that his car had been involved in an accident," he said. "He hit a police car!"

"Sometimes the sun just shines down on us," Roberts said. "Even in Oregon. Our guy OK?"

"It was Faye Simmons on patrol. She was just shaken up, thank God. She was chasing the suspect's car because it had smashed into a vehicle and failed to stop. She'd backed off on the pursuit because they were moving into a more congested area."

"I bet I can guess the rest."

"Right," Pfeifer said. "As Simmons slowed, the hit-and-run suspect sped up and ran the red light. Crump's lucky he and the other driver weren't killed."

"Let's wait until we interview the guy before you pull the protection team back from the beach," Roberts advised.

"Satin pillows are a <u>smashing</u> success in any master bedroom."

30

Pfeifer called Russell Graham to let him know that they had a possible suspect in custody. He followed that phone conversation with a call to Laura's cell phone.

"I'm calling to report an automobile accident in downtown Portland," Pfeifer told her.

It'd have to be in Portland, Laura thought. We don't have a 'downtown' in Yachats.

"Were the drivers anyone I know? Were they hurt?" she asked.

"A car that blew through a red light matches the vehicle description you gave us of the car you saw leaving the scene on the day of your bank robbery."

"For the last time, it wasn't *my* bank robbery," she said in exasperation.

"*The* bank robbery," he corrected himself. "And its license plate matches that of a vehicle seen in your neighborhood by one of your Neighborhood Watch ladies the same date that the intruder was in your kitchen."

"Were there injuries?"

"Surprisingly, the driver who had the green light to proceed into the intersection wasn't badly hurt. She was alert and appeared to have minor injuries," he said. "She was transported to the hospital to be evaluated."

"And, the other driver?"

"Due to be transported downtown to us."

"You got the S.O.B.!"

"Laura Howard!" he said in mock surprise.

"You misheard. What I actually said was 'thank you, Detective. Thank you ever so much.'"

He chuckled. "We'll be in touch later to ask you if you can identify this guy. For now, I think you can rest a little easier," he said.

"Can we start home?"

"It'd be after dark by the time you got here," he said. "I'm going to call and give Pete a credit card number. Why don't you two join Pete and Jamie at The Drift Inn for dinner, compliments of the Portland Police Bureau? Then you and Esther can start home tomorrow in daylight. We'll let Pete and Jaimie stay on the job throughout the night and during tomorrow's drive until we can figure out who was flashing your photo over there."

"So I'm not the only one who thinks Photo Guy is a little creepy?" Laura asked.

"That would be a positive," he said and hung up.

PETE TOOK the wheel of the Taurus and drove north to Lincoln City and then cut over to Salem. Esther rode with bodyguard Jamie. Laura knew Jamie and Esther were less than a mile behind them, bringing up the rear.

Both cars arrived in Portland near dinner time and Russ greeted Esther and Laura at the door of The Harrington. The smells of a home cooked dinner—chili and hot bread?—wafted toward the door. Laura tried not to think about what her kitchen must look like with Russ at the helm. He helped them out of their coats and seated them at the dining room table where they filled him in on their surprise trip to the coast.

Russ opened a can of tuna for Louise.

THEIR POLICE ESCORTS parked up the block where they could observe the house through the night.

Jaimie and Pete checked in with Detectives Pfeifer and Roberts, who had no further reports about the unknown person who had been showing Laura's photo to merchants on the Oregon coast.

"There's reason they're called 'starving artists.' Their work should only be featured on motel room walls."

31

The driver of the mangled black car had been belligerent since he was put in a Portland patrol car at the scene of the accident. Two officers joined the medical crew in the ambulance that arrived to transport him to the hospital.

Pfeifer still marveled that the man had walked away from the collision with only minor cuts on his arms. Those injuries were sustained when he tried to exit the car through the broken driver's side window, planning to flee the scene.

The suspect might have disappeared in the confusion following that accident if a patrol car hadn't already been in pursuit. Bystanders made sure he didn't leave until that police unit pulled up.

Pfeifer suspected those bystanders might not have been so vigilant had they known the length of Crump's rap sheet. He appreciated their support.

DETECTIVES PFEIFER and Roberts sat in on the interview of the suspect.

"Say, just say, I *was* driving past when there was a bank robbery," Crump said. "That doesn't make me a party to what was going on inside."

"There's an eye witness."

"Yeah? What can she tell you? That I was driving too fast?"

"How'd you know the witness was a woman?"

"Don't try to confuse me," Crump said. "I know how you guys operate."

"Then, you probably also know that later today we'll have the person who saw you at the scene of the bank heist—and later up close in the kitchen—here to ID you."

"She'll be lying if she said I was the one that did those things."

"Again with the feminine pronoun," Roberts said.

Crump looked confused.

"What *things* are we talking about?" Pfeifer asked.

"The other jerk who was in here earlier . . ."

"The other *detective*," Pfeifer corrected him.

"The other detective," Crump repeated. "He was trying to get me to cop to being some kind of a pervert."

"And?"

"And, do you think a good-looking guy like me would stoop to being a Peeping Tom?"

"You stooped to being a flower killer," Roberts said. He admitted to Pfeifer later that the statement may have been was one of the dumbest things he'd ever said when interviewing a suspect, but it worked.

"So what if I misjudged the width of the road and wiped out her precious garden?" Crump asked. "Tell her to try Miracle Grow."

"You really don't know when to keep your mouth shut," Pfeifer said. "You might want to work on that before you go to prison."

"I know all about you guys and your methods. I watch a lot of movies. I know how they used tire tread marks to free Joe Pesci's cousin. I've watched *My Cousin Vinny* twenty times. Trust me. Your so-called witness ain't no Marisa Tormei."

"Identifying tire treads that way seldom works now that most tires are mass produced," Pfeifer said. He wasn't sure that was true, but he thought he'd throw the suspect a curve. "You still driving the Scion?"

"So what if I am?"

Pfeifer had all the information he needed from this interview. Crump had admitted to being at the scene of the bank robbery and driving the car spotted speeding away from the area. He had implied that he knew the resident at The Harrington, though stopped short this time of admitting that he'd held her hostage in her kitchen. Then, for good measure, he'd copped to one of the vandalism charges. They'd put him in a lineup and then schedule a second interview.

Pfeifer almost felt sorry Crump. The suspect had turned down the offer to have an attorney represent him. They'd asked him that at the scene of the accident, again when he arrived at the Police Bureau, and twice more during the interview.

"It's a home, not a movie set. Sometimes comfort trumps design."

32

Russell Graham breathed a heavy sigh of relief when he heard that the police had a suspect in custody.

"The man's admitted to being at the scene of the bank job and to some of the vandalism at Laura's home," Pfeifer told Russ in a brief update by phone. "I think she can relax. This guy's not coming back to Portland for a long time."

Maybe Russ could relax now too. The two men who broke into Esther's place had been in custody and were now out of state in lockdown at a drug rehabilitation facility. Now, the guy who'd run Laura off the road was out of circulation as well.

He sighed heavily. Watching out for Laura Howard was not a job for the faint of heart.

Laura had only been back in Portland for a few hours when she phoned Russ to let him know that she and Esther were driving downtown to view a police lineup.

On the way to the Police Bureau she worried that she might not remember what the man who had helped himself to a snack and her steak knife looked like. What if she couldn't recognize him?

Pfeifer and Roberts escorted her to a small room. Neither one of them said a word once the light came on behind the one-way glass and the men filed in. She looked at each of the six men twice. She had no doubt when she pointed to Crump. "Fourth one from the left," she said. "For sure."

PFEIFER HAD now reviewed the report from the officers who returned from their assignment watching Laura and Esther at the coast. He was as uneasy as they were about whoever had flashed the photo of Laura. If it truly was a picture of Laura. Could the clerk have made up the incident he reported? They all doubted that.

Pfeifer worried that Laura didn't seem to be all that concerned about the grocery clerk's report.

ESTHER HADN'T SEEN the tiny house yet, and Laura promised that both of them would stop out there after they left the police station. Maybe that would soothe Esther's hurt feelings for not being asked to witness the lineup.

They parked in front of the tiny house and got out of the recently repaired truck. Russ was there waiting for them.

Laura stood perfectly still, staring at the little house.

"Something's different here," she told Russ.

While they talked, Esther was circling the compact home for the third time, each time exclaiming about the paint colors as she made her rounds.

"You spotted the change?" Russ asked Laura. "I added a foot in each direction to the sunroom. It's a 'tack on' anyway so it didn't alter the main footprint."

"Good idea."

"Better than you may realize," he said. "It gives enough added space to build in bunk beds."

"I always wanted bunk beds when I was a kid."

"A toddler will fit on the lower one now. And when he's in grade school, he can crack his head open leaping off the top bunk playing Superman."

"The voice of experience?" Laura asked.

"Could be."

"Residents of plastic ant farms are the ideal pets for owners of a tiny house."

33

"Do you ever think about how one unexpected event can trigger all kinds of disaster?" Laura asked.

"You thinking about geophysics? Like one small pebble starting a landslide?" Russ asked.

"I can honestly tell you I've *never* thought about geophysics. Not once in my entire life. I was thinking about a drive to the bank. All I wanted to do that morning was give my new cream suit an outing, cash a refund check, and find out about lower mortgage rates."

"That's *three* small things," Esther said.

"So you think everything since then has been tied to mortgage rates?" Russ asked.

"Or payback for vanity. It was too early in the year to wear that suit. I knew it at the time."

"If fashion mistakes trigger Karma, I'm in big trouble," Esther said. She shifted in her chair adjusting the plush magenta jogging suit she was wearing with plaid tennis shoes.

The three of them were seated at the work table at Graham Construction reviewing the events of the past two or three months. The conversation was triggered by Esther's new concern for "gaining closure," the latest television catch phrase she'd picked up from Dr. Phil.

"You remember I have this completion complex, don't you?" Esther asked.

The other two nodded. Esther was the one who couldn't leave work late afternoons until she had sent the last invoice and tidied her desk top.

"I want to make sure Laura's safe now."

"I feel fine," Laura said.

"That's you! *I* need to 'feel fine.'"

"Let's humor her," Russ said. "She baked the banana bread for break time."

"Ready?" Esther asked.

The other two nodded.

"The bank robbers are behind bars."

"Check," they said in unison.

"Bernie and Clyde are locked up either in jail or in rehab," Esther said.

242

"Check," they repeated.

"Rolando's murderer Crump was the same one who was in Laura's kitchen. He caused the vandalism at her place and drove the get-away car at the bank."

Russ nodded. "And he held her at gunpoint in her kitchen."

"Plus he sideswiped Laura's truck and could have killed her," Esther said. "I just changed my mind on capital punishment."

"Check," Laura said, hoping they could avoid a long discussion on the death penalty.

"No check from me," Russ said. "I won't be able to mark him off in *my* list until we hear his sentence."

"Agreed."

"Just for fun, Laura, what would you do if you walked in on another bank robbery?" he asked.

"I know what I'd do," Esther said before Laura could speak. "Switch to online banking."

There was a quiet knock at the front door and Laura bounced up to see who had arrived.

The woman at the door introduced herself as Catherine Denham. Laura had never met her before and noticed that she was much younger than neighbor Vance Denham. Perhaps twenty to twenty-five years younger. His wife? A daughter?

She invited the woman to step inside, but Catherine Denham preferred to speak to Laura alone on the porch.

"There's something I've got to get off my chest," she said.

She looked down at her feet, then looked up, met Laura's eye, and launched into an apology at great length for having entered The Harrington during the February snowstorm and left what she described as a "juvenile note."

"My husband and I thought you were selling drugs," she said. "I'm so embarrassed and so sorry."

She handed Laura a plate of cookies.

"I'd understand if you wanted to report me for breaking and entering or something, but you left the door unlocked."

"I left in a hurry the night of the snowstorm. I double check all my door locks any time I leave now."

"They're brownies," Catherine Denham said as she looked down at the cookies.

"How do I know they're not laced with marijuana?" Laura asked.

The woman looked like she'd been slapped.

"Pay back," Laura said. "I'm teasing you, Mrs. Denham. I accept your apology. You thought you were

244

protecting the neighborhood when you left that note. Believe me, I accept your apology," Laura repeated.

She stopped short of asking the woman to join the others inside.

Laura stepped back inside and told Esther and Russ what Mrs. Denham had said.

"I wouldn't trust her," Esther said. "Think about it. She not only knew when your house was empty and we were all bunking at Graham Construction, she also knew that all three of us were here today. Doesn't that make you wonder?"

"It didn't until you mentioned it," Laura said.

"I say we eat her brownies and mull it over."

"Blue and white checked fabric left the style scene in 1958. Let's leave it wherever it went."

34

One of the new-hires at the Bureau walked toward the detective's desk. Leonard Roberts didn't look up from his paperwork. He didn't have time for a "meet and greet" today

"Detective Roberts, you got a minute?"

"Half."

"We kept at it and we were able to ID the phantom grocery shopper in Yachats. The one who was sought in the Howard case."

"And?" Roberts prompted.

"He's a flunky who was hired by that local woman TV newscaster," he said. "You know her. The one with the legs and the tight sweaters."

"Good to know the money the Bureau spent for sensitivity and anti-harassment training was a success with you."

"I 'm as sensitive as the next guy. I just can't think of the babe's name."

"I rest my case."

TV NEWSWOMAN Candace Galassi agreed to come to the Police Bureau to talk with Detectives Roberts and Pfeifer.

They exchanged introductions and handshakes and she began reciting the list of past broadcasting awards and citations of excellence she had received for her reporting.

Roberts interrupted her.

"Were you in Yachats last weekend?"

"Not I," she said coyly. She crossed her legs and leaned forward. "I'm ready for your next question," she said.

"Did you contact either Laura Howard, Russell Graham, Esther Graham or Ernie Gallo within the past two months?" Pfeifer asked.

"I don't know an Esther Graham," she said.

"Answer the question," Roberts ordered.

"You two do know that we have a first amendment to the Constitution, don't you?   And, that it specifically includes freedom of the press?"

"Familiar with that," Roberts said.   "And, I'm sure you're familiar with obstruction of justice."

"You don't have to be threatening about this," she said.

"Have you been harassing these people in an attempt to get an interview?" Roberts asked

"No. Not harassing."

"Have you contacted any of them more than four times during that time period?" he asked next.

"Yes. That's what I do for a living."

"Well, what you do for a living could have gotten them killed that weekend," Pfeifer said.

MS. GALASSI admitted that she had hired her brother-in-law to scope out Oregon coastal towns when she hadn't been able to reach any of the partners at Graham Construction by phone.

"Did it occur to you, ma'am, that they might have intentionally blocked your calls?"

"Of course. So I drove down the street where they live and I didn't see any sign of life."

"Go on."

"So, I said to myself, 'Candace, where would you go on a nice weekend like this?'" she said. "'The coast' I answered me. I was scheduled to be 'on air' for that Saturday night's newscast. So I hired Denny."

"Denny would be?"

"My ex-brother-in-law," she said. "Denny started driving early morning in Astoria, had lunch in Newport, and finished the hunt in Gold Beach. He got nothing."

"He could have gotten Laura Howard killed."

Ms. Galassi looked serious for the first time. "That wasn't the plan. I wouldn't hurt a flea."

"It's a fly," Pfeifer said absently.

"Your behavior put two citizens and two law officers at risk. That behavior forced them to flee at high speed from Yachats to Portland."

"But, Denny never found them. I bought his lunch and gas and paid him fifty bucks for nothing."

"We don't plan to file any charges," Pfeifer said. Mainly because there was no way charges would stand up in court, he thought. "But, we'd like to ask your cooperation."

"Of course, Detective."

"If you should need to talk with Laura Howard or the Grahams, could you please call me in advance? You understand, we can't require you to do that, but I'd like to be there with you when you talk with them."

"That'd be lovely," she said. "Though, I think that bank robbery incident is kind of old news by now. Maybe dinner?"

"Our work schedules may not be compatible for that," Pfeifer said and eased toward the door.

"Nut case," he said under his breath as he left.

PFEIFER PHONED the Graham Construction office to update Laura on the recent developments. She wasn't available, but he decided no one would question him if he left the information with Esther Graham.

"We made a classic error in assuming that the same person was responsible for everything that happened after the event at the bank," Pfeifer said. "And *I* should have known better."

"Don't beat yourself up," Esther told him. "Laura's the only one in town who's allowed to deck somebody."

"You can cover dings on wood furniture by rubbing an unshelled walnut across the scarred area."

35

Laura arrived at work early. She'd felt safer there than in her own home the last few weeks. It'd take time, she knew, to feel at ease again at The Harrington. She had explained that to Louise this morning.

"There's a phone message from Detective Roberts for you," Russ said. "He wants you to call him back."

"Why didn't he call me at home?"

"Probably because he left the message at 3 a.m."

"Those guys work weird hours," Laura said. "Didn't their parents ever tell them that nothing good happens after midnight?"

"Never heard that one," Russ said. "It could explain the strange shifts police work."

"When I was a teenager," she said, "That was the standard parental justification for a midnight curfew."

"For girls, maybe."

"I'm almost afraid to call Roberts," Laura said. "He's not the friendliest guy on the force."

"Would you be if you worked those hours?"

LAURA WAITED until lunch time to relay the message from Detective Roberts to Russ and Esther.

"They picked up my Peeping Tom," she said.

"After all these weeks?" Esther asked.

"I didn't know the guy was back" Russ said. "You two need to keep me up to date."

"As far as we knew he hadn't returned," Esther said.

"It seems I wasn't the only one Mr. Peeper was watching," Laura said. "The police nabbed them across town looking into a woman's townhouse. Only this time, they tried a higher window and fell into a climbing rosebush."

"Them?" Russ and Esther asked together.

"Get this. They've arrested the bank security guard and his *wife.*"

"When you and I were going through our list of possible suspects," Esther said, "I asked about anybody you'd met at the bank. You described the bank guard as a friendly sawed-off little guy who couldn't possibly wear a size 14 shoe."

"He doesn't."

"So give," Esther said. "What else did Roberts say?"

"Mr. Peeper still had on a large walking cast from the gun accident at the bank. That's the print the cops found. The print was embedded in the mud because he was balancing his wife on his shoulders so *she* could look inside."

"Talk about sick," Russ said.

"The cops think they're pretty much harmless," Laura said. "Roberts said he talked to Mr. and Mrs. Thomas separately. Both of them claim Frank Thomas was obsessed with guilt. He knew he'd failed the teller and me the day of the bank heist and he couldn't let it go."

"He should have felt guilty," Russ said. "He didn't do his job."

"The guy couldn't sleep at night, and, according to the wife, he dwelled on the subject day in and day out, Roberts said. The two told Roberts they started going past both the teller and my houses late at night to make sure we were safe."

"A little far-fetched," Esther said. "Wasn't there an elderly lady at the bank that day too? I don't hear anything about the bank guard peeking in on *her*. Like always, just the shapely, young ones get protection. I protest."

"Detective Roberts had the same thoughts," Laura said. "But, then Mrs. Thomas produced a log book where she had recorded the dates and times they'd made security checks at each of our residences at bi-weekly intervals. . . "

"Bi-weekly? You're starting to talk like a cop," Russ said.

"Roberts thinks the Thomases are—in his words—'peculiar and quirky, but safe.'"

"The old P and Q defense," Esther said under her breath.

"What happens to them now?" Russ asked. "Were they arrested?"

"They were charged with trespassing, harassment, stalking, and criminal voyeurism. Plus, the arresting officer added 'tampering with a witness' for good measure," she added.

"I'd have thrown in a charge of first degree lunacy." Esther said.

"The cops cited them and then drove them home. The bank guard may have re-injured his foot when the two of them hit the ground. His wife, Nelda, complained of shoulder pain, but they both refused to be transported to a hospital," Laura reported.

"And, it gets worse," she added. "Detective Roberts and Pfeifer are going to grill Thomas again about his whereabouts also over this past weekend. They've sent someone out to his house to see if there is any evidence of beach sand on the tires on his SUV."

"That's way over the line if he followed the guys assigned to stay behind you en route to the beach."

"We would have looked like a Cuban conga line," Esther said. "Us, the bodyguards' car, and then the idiot bank security guy's vehicle bringing up the rear."

"I don't care how many years he worked as a guard," Russ said. "Who does that? He sounds like he's got a screw loose. Isn't this the same whacko who put a bullet through his foot?"

"One in the same," Laura said. "I asked about the notes the Thomas team had taken. I'm not wild about having a log of my daily life floating around at the Police Bureau."

"I'm with you on that," Esther said.

"I had Pfeifer read some of the entries to me," Laura said.

"And?"

Laura repeated those entries that she could recall.

- *Orange, mature cat appears irritable and restless.*

- *Exterior windows need a good washing.*

- *Firewood supply running low.*

"They couldn't do better than that?" Russ asked.

"Risqué, right?" Laura said, and continued to recite.

- *Lights remained on after 12:30 a.m.*

- *Same two occupants. Cat stretching.*

- *Subject in blue plaid bathrobe and fuzzy pink slippers.*

"You little slut," Esther said.

"If the entries don't get any hotter than that, I think you're OK," Russ said.

"Do you have to appear in court?" Esther asked.

"I opted out."

"Good. I'd rather go to the trial for the bank robber." Esther said. "There may be TV crews at that one."

"Awkward angles on home exteriors can be hidden by a carefully placed climbing rose bush. Mlle. Cecile Brunner is a good choice."

36

Esther was fifteen minutes late for work at Graham Construction. This was unusual considering her twenty step commute to the job site. Laura asked Russ if he thought they should check on her, but he suggested they give Aunt Esther another ten minutes to arrive. Maybe she was attending to some last minute details before tomorrow's wedding.

When Esther came in the side door at Graham Construction five minutes later, she had Ernie in tow.

"I'm glad you're both here," Ernie said. "It'll save us telling you separately."

"Telling us what?" Russ asked.

"Esther and I have cancelled our wedding."

"Done *what*?" Laura asked.

"We've decided to shack up instead," Esther said.

259

"Aunt Esther!"

"Let me rephrase that, dear," Ernie told Esther. "My sweet Esther and I have decided to meld our social security checks into one account and skip the formalities of a wedding at our ages."

"But we have guests coming. We have flowers. We all bought new clothes," Laura protested.

Russ bent down on one knee, keeping his balance with the help of the fingers on his left hand placed strategically on the floor.

"Are you OK?" Laura asked.

"Never better." He withdrew a small box from his pocket with his free hand. He snapped the box open and watched as the sunlight pouring through the windows glanced off the ring.

Laura's mouth fell open. "Is that the ring I admired when I shopped with Ernie?" she asked.

"Quiet. I'm the only one who's asking questions today," he said, grinning. "Laura, will you marry me?"

Laura was stunned into silence.

"Once again, I'm not sure if that's a 'yes' or 'no,'" Russ said. "But, wait! There's more."

Laura stood quietly, too dazed to speak.

"Laura Howard, will you marry me?"

"Yes."

"Tomorrow?" he asked.

"Tomorrow?"

"Tomorrow," he repeated.

"Yes!"

"You obviously knew best," Ernie whispered to Esther.

"Of course I did," she said.

Laura looked at the three smiling conspirators standing across from her.

"I smell a rat," she said.

"Perhaps a small mouse," Ernie offered.

"Esther talked me into buying that beautiful pastel dress that I worried was too bridal for a matron of honor. Was this plot already hatched then?"

"It's a perfect choice for the younger bride," Esther said smugly. "It's the color of a pale vanilla custard pie."

"And, Ernie, saw me admiring rings?"

"You said you liked a simple one," Ernie recalled. "I drove our man Russ to that store the next day and he liked the same one."

"We figured that was a good omen," Russ said.

Ernie gave Russ a conspiratorial pat on the back. "If you don't mind," he said, "I've got some cooking to do before tomorrow when guests show up."

"Guests. I forgot the guests," Laura said.

"I don't know how you could have forgotten them," Russ said. "You and I made the guest list the night that Esther claimed that tending to all the details of planning a wedding gave her a headache."

"And I advised her to carry a nosegay."

"Damn!" Russ said. "I ordered Kansas sunflowers and white baby's breath."

"They'll go beautifully with the pale yellow gown," impromptu wedding coordinator Esther said.

"Ernie and I both bought new suits," Russ reminded Laura.

"And, Esther's baking *our* favorite cake," Laura said. She looked accusingly at Russ.

"Don't look at me. This was obviously more than a one man job."

"Did you honestly think I'd marry Ernie when our monogram would have been E and E?" Esther asked. "We'd have sounded like a Stop 'n Shop."

"Backyard studios diminish the divorce rate while enhancing the landscape."

37

The bride wore her auburn hair in an upswept style with a simple pearled clip securing the shoulder-length veil. The small group gathered to hear the vows watched as she maneuvered past the garden planters, her pale yellow gown narrowly missing the rough wood braces for the trellis.

The bridegroom looked dapper in a dark suit. They both smiled as the minister began the ceremony.

"Dearly Beloved," he said.

"Who's 'dearly beloved?'" Esther asked a little too loudly.

"You are, dear," Ernie told her. "Now let the man talk."

There was a quiet titter from the small group seated in the folding chairs set up on the neatly trimmed patch of grass to the side of the gazebo behind The Harrington.

Reverend Stanley Baker continued as though there had been no interruption. "We're here today to share the joy with these two as they are joined in holy matrimony." He turned back to Laura and Russ who stood before him holding hands.

"Who giveth this bride?" the minister asked.

"I do," Ernie said.

"Your relationship to the bride, sir?"

"Tile layer."

There was a quiet chuckle from one of the guests in the front row.

"Works for me," the minister said.

Esther leaned over and gave Ernie a kiss on the cheek.

"Do you, Laura Howard, promise to take Russell Patrick Graham to be your wedded husband?"

"I . . ."

"Not yet," the minister said quietly. "Do you, Laura, promise to love, to cherish, to honor, to obey, forsaking all others," he continued. "In sickness as well as in health, in adversity as well as in prosperity, for better or

264

for worse as long as you both shall live?" He stopped to catch his breath.

"And," he began again, "do you further promise to clean all your own paint brushes and to make no changes in design after city or county building permits have been issued."

Laura stood silently, considering the questions carefully.

There was an uneasy silence.

"I'm OK with everything but 'obey,'" she said.

Best man Ernie turned to Russ. "Close enough?" he asked.

"Close enough," Russ repeated.

"Then, I do," Laura said.

Russ gave her hand a squeeze.

The minister looked at Russ. "And, you, Sir," he said. "Do you promise to love, to cherish, to honor Laura, forsaking all others, in sickness and in health, in adversity as well as in prosperity, for better or for worse, and to cleave only to her so long as you both shall live?" Russ opened his mouth to speak, but was stopped short.

"Not so fast," Reverend Baker said.

Russ waited silently.

"And, do you, Russell Graham, also promise to love the lovely Laura from this day forward, no matter how many times the furniture is rearranged and the walls repainted?"

"I do. I definitely do."

Baker cleared his throat. "Is there anyone present who objects to the marriage of this couple?"

Chris Pfeifer and Leonard Roberts stood up. "We object," they said in unison.

"You *what?*" the bride asked.

Reverend Baker signaled Laura to remain quiet. He grinned at the two police officers.

"Please state your objection," he said.

Roberts nodded to Pfeifer who spoke for the two of them. "We wish to amend the vows yet another time," he said.

"How now?" the minister asked, sounding like an owl in a children's book. He wiped the sweat beads from his forehead. He was enjoying the warm informality of this wedding, but he had never officiated at a wedding where there was an objection.

"We're OK with 'love, honor' and all that," Pfeifer said, "but, we propose adding 'and keep the Portland Police Bureau number on speed dial," he said.

Officers Daniels and Ryan spoke next. "We second that."

"I see," said the reverend solemnly. He looked at the almost-wed couple standing before him.

Russ and Laura nodded agreement and repeated the amended vows.

"If there are no further objections . . ." Baker crossed his fingers behind his back and waited only ten seconds.

"I now pronounce you husband and wife. Or, wife and husband. Or, whatever suits you two. This is Oregon."

He plopped down in the folding chair behind him and watched with the others while the newlyweds exchanged a discreet kiss.

"We'll save the good stuff for later," Russ whispered to his bride.

The minister rose again and spoke to the guests. "The bridegroom's Aunt Esther tells me you are all invited to join the happy couple in the culinary delight of a lifetime," he said. "Best man Ernie's gift to us all."

"There's one other thing," Esther said. "The bride and groom can't sneak out until they've admired the wedding cake." Esther stepped to the serving table and pointed to a modest-sized three-layer cake decorated with *butter cream* lattice work on *fondant* icing. Miniature figures of an orange cat and a sheep dog, each molded of colored *marzipan,* peeked from under the scalloped edge of the cake.

Ernie gave the toast, Esther cut the cake, and Mr. and Mrs. Russell Graham slipped out the back gate after the last guest wished them well.

A tiny cake was waiting for them on a tiny table at a tiny house.

"There's room for spontaneity in both love and decor."—Laura Graham, Interior Decorator

Afterword

- Russell and Laura Graham now live at the Portland construction company headquarters on weekdays and spend their weekends and work furloughs at the tiny house near the pond.

- Rolando's widow Cecelia accepted Laura's offer to live rent-free at The Harrington where there's room for the Hernandez children to romp inside on winter days. Laura's happy that the house is occupied and not a magnet for vandals.

- Esther Graham continues to be an active member of Neighborhood Watch group. She's started a dog-walking business to fill the hours she doesn't spend on bookkeeping tasks at Graham Construction. Her new business venture, the Woof 'n Poops, turned a profit for the first time last month.

- Mickey Crump remains incarcerated at a maximum security prison after being sentenced under Oregon's Measure 11 guidelines. And, would-be bank robber John Smith resides at a separate corrections facility where he is studying law at the prison library.

Acknowledgments

Many thanks to book club members who selected the Designer Mysteries for their reading lists . . . I haven't met you all, but I like that you like character Laura Howard and the gang. Maryland club member Sandee advised me that there comes a time when characters either need to be wed or dead. So sad. So true.

Without long-time friend, computer whiz, and editor Kitty Buchner, the manuscript would still be stored under the bed. It's hard to read under there.

Neighbor Michael keeps me laughing and in the right mood to create silly decorating tips. She also waters my garden when I'm absorbed in a project and forget that plants, like characters in a mystery, can drop dead when one least expects it.

Special thanks to my sister Margie who reads first drafts and sets me straight when I've wandered too far afield. Margie created the title *Studs, Tools, and Fools* and found the cover art. She's as sharp and spunky as that cat on the cover.

Author

Kathleen Hering and her husband divide their time between Jacksonville and Albany, Oregon, where she writes from the painted wood desk in the kitchen. She started writing fiction after retiring from public schools as a middle school principal and personnel director. She is married to noted print journalist and TV and radio news commentator Hasso Hering. They spend their leisure time riding a tandem bicycle, rowing a tippy canoe on the Willamette River, and enjoying their grandchildren—not necessarily in that order.

Readers can contact author Kathleen Hering at _designermysteries@gmail.com_.

Designer Mystery Series

Hammered, Nailed and Screwed

Oregon interior decorator Laura Howard is receiving messages from her husband on her telephone answering machine. It's his voice all right. But his ashes are in the urn on Laura's fireplace mantel . . .

Ripped, Stripped and Flipped

Laura Howard does not intend to keep the gift someone left for her in the yard of the 19th Century Italianate house she's restoring. And, detectives don't plan to close their investigation until they find out who delivered the gift, a corpse wrapped in newly poured concrete.

Studs, Tools and Fools

Interior Decorator Laura Howard had her life planned down to the last piece of designer drapery fabric. That was before she made that ill-fated trip downtown and landed smack dab in the middle of a bank heist. Now instead of juggling fabric swatches and designing dream kitchens, she's dodging threats and dealing with a cop a day at the Portland Police Bureau. Will she ever have the serene life she and her long-time business partner had planned together?

67295065R00168

Made in the USA
Middletown, DE
20 March 2018